Cracks in the Ice

Cheimon Tales #1
Nicole Dennis

Table of Contents

Blurb:

Frost scion, Jacob Serac, recognizes something is wrong in his relationship with his crystal partner, Devyn Risher. Things go wrong when he abducts Devyn for a weekend getaway. After contacting a reindeer agent from the Cheimon Patrol Division, the situation darkens and alerts to even more problems.

The truth emerges along with adventures, mishaps, and chaos. Jacob, Devyn, and the Cheimon try to save their home and lives from the looming dark magic disaster. Can all this happen during Winter Solstice? It's the highlight of the North Pole Dimension's year.

Can Jacob and Devyn heal their relationship and seal the cracks in Jacob's crystal heart?

FatCat Books Ink

The author acknowledges the trademarked status and owners of the following word marks used in this story:

Montblanc: *Montblanc International*

Zoom: *Zoom Video Communications, Inc.*

Chapter One

With everything prepared, now the plan needed to be executed. The plan laid out, somewhat rehearsed, and ready.

The only piece missing was Devyn. As usual.

"Chill. Chill. It's why you're taking this step. To give this relationship one last chance before your heart cracks even worse. You felt the splinters. This must happen if you want to keep your humanity. You know why you must do this to Devyn," Jacob Serac muttered. He moved his hand across the messenger bag's strap in a soothing pattern to calm the craziness happening within his head. Then he paced a couple of times across the hardwood floor. His steps changed from the tapping on the hardwood to the soft cushion of the expensive Persian area rug that decorated the waiting area of Devyn Risher's office. At this point, he didn't care if his boots messed up the fibers. His fingers tingled while his frost magic rose with his anxiety.

"Jacob, I apologize for the delay. Devyn is finishing the conference call, but there's another meeting scheduled," Devyn's assistant, Mia, said when she stepped out of Devyn's corner office.

"Did he know I would be here this afternoon?"

"Yes, I put it on his calendar and warned him, but..." She shrugged and stopped next to her desk.

"He either ignored the request or added something."

"Exactly. I'm so sorry, Jacob."

"This weekend away must happen, Mia. It's important for me and I need Devyn to be present and not preoccupied with the office. Can you—"

"Clear his calendar for Friday and the weekend? I already did, but there are times when he schedules his own appointments if he notices some free spaces. I'm sorry, Jacob, but I don't know if it'll happen."

Jacob shook his head. "No. Not going to accept his excuses or workaholic nature this time. Clear things again. Find someone to cover his meeting. Please. If this weekend doesn't happen, then..." He shrugged. "It's over. We're over."

Your time in humanity is over for the next century, Frost. That's the gist of the problem. Last heart. Last chance. If you shatter... No heart. No life. Just ice.

Mia nibbled on her inner lower lip and glanced at the door. "I don't know if I should interfere like that. Especially with him."

"Please, Mia. This weekend is vital. I wouldn't ask for the help if I didn't mean it."

She checked the phone system and nodded. "Go now. He's off the line. Go. I'll take care of the rest and lock him out of the calendar. He's not going to leave without a nasty fight."

"I'll manage him. I promise to not let you feel the heat for anything that happens because of his disappearance. Thank you." Jacob hugged her quick and rushed toward the door. He pushed open the door to the expansive corner office Devyn Risher achieved within seven years. It was an incredible achievement, but the entire time Jacob felt there was something off about the way it happened. "Devyn, we need to—"

"Jacob, look, I know you were coming here for something, but we'll have to reschedule. I have to get this meeting with Tokyo overseen," Devyn interrupted in a brusque tone. He signed different pieces of paper with an elegant Montblanc pen Jacob gifted him one Winter Solstice. He pushed the fingers of his free hand through his sunflower blond hair. He tried to sweep back his bangs, but the locks fell back across his forehead and covered his dark blue eyes.

Did Devyn even remember that Solstice or where he received the pen? At least he uses it so that helps to renew the connection. Though that's not the piece I'm concerned about for the link between us.

"Someone else will hold the meeting. Mia is changing everything. You need to come with me. Now," Jacob said while he pulled a small bundle from a pocket. He unwrapped the end and moved around the massive ebony wood desk.

Devyn gave him no other choice, but to use this bundle. It wasn't how Jacob wanted things to happen.

"That's impossible. No one else can manage it. I'll get with you another—" Devyn paused when Jacob stood next to him.

Jacob caught a quick flash of something dark shadow Devyn's eyes when he moved closer. *Oh, yes, there is something else within my Devyn. Something deep in his heart that is trying to control him and pull him away from me.*

"What are you doing?"

"I'm so sorry, but this must happen. I need you to come with me and you're not being very cooperative." Jacob tapped his fist against Devyn's neck. He sent a small burst of magic to activate things.

"Ow!" Devyn pressed his fingers to his stinging neck. He rose to his feet and moved to get away from Jacob's reach. Then he stopped and shook his head. "What the hell—"

Jacob opened his hand and stared at the unusually shaped needle filled with the sparkling combination of holly berry, mistletoe, chamomile, and lavender. A kind of special winter drug cocktail he ordered from the R&D elves at the North Pole Dimension workshop. He hoped the crazy concoction could assist him with this crazy plan. He glanced again at Devyn, who stood straight and still.

A little too still.

"Devyn?"

A long slow blink of those deep blue eyes responded to his name.

"Speak to me."

"Hello, Jacob."

"Oh, blast the icicles. Could this stuff be too powerful for a mortal? I could have sworn I specified to R&D that he is mortal on my request. Frozen balls, this isn't good." Jacob nibbled on his lower lip. "Crapshoot of icicles. Crap."

"Okay. I will go to the bathroom and crap." Devyn turned to walk off to the bathroom attached to his office.

"Whoa. Stop. No."

Devyn stopped.

Jacob swallowed hard. *Okay. Going to have to reconsider how I use my words and required responses.* "Devyn, I need you to place your laptop, charger, pen, cell phone, wallet, and keys in your briefcase. Now. Then you will close and lock the briefcase. We're going to leave the office."

"Yes, Jacob," Devyn said while he returned to his desk and placed the required items in the briefcase. He closed and locked it. Then he waited.

Freaky. Hope it wears off soon. If not, I need to call in reinforcements to figure out what is happening to him. Please let there be a reversal.

"Put on your coat and scarf. It's cold outside."

With a nod, Devyn followed the new orders.

"Now take your briefcase and follow me. A car is waiting for us downstairs. We have a journey to take."

Without saying anything, Devyn picked up his briefcase and followed Jacob out of the vast corner office.

Mia watched them walk to the elevator. Her jaw dropped when Devyn didn't say anything to her or even look at her. "Umm... Jacob?"

Jacob held up his hand and shook his head. "Thank you, Mia. He'll be back in the office on Monday, but we'll be out of cell and WiFi range. If anything changes, I'll find a way to contact you." He hit the button on the elevator.

"Good luck," she said.

Jacob glanced at the quiet Devyn. "I need it."

When the doors closed, Jacob flicked his fingers to cover the camera in a light frost for secrecy with what he needed to do next. The frost would melt as soon as he left the vicinity and alter the recordings enough, so no one would investigate their sudden disappearance. Hopefully, the security team would place the blame on a computer glitch and not question anything or investigate further. That's usually what happens when mortals are near his magic. With their escape covered, he pulled a miniature glass snow globe from another pocket. He rolled it between his fingers to activate the magic. He whispered the destination and tossed the globe into the corner.

A blue swirl opened when the globe cracked and released the magic.

Jacob grabbed Devyn's arm and tugged him through the portal.

The swirl closed behind them and disappeared in a bit of sparkly dust and snowflakes.

Instead of going to their gorgeous Jeffries Point condominium in the East Boston area, Jacob knew they required something more private. They entered Jacob's cabin on a secluded island off the Canadian coast. This cabin was his power base for the entire coast. He conferred with all the Flakes, Verglas and Ice elves and fairies who helped him organize and control the chaos that was a winter system. His area was far too large for him to control alone and the NP Division organized the FVI Department to assist all the Frosts.

Devyn thought it was a pleasant get-away cabin that Jacob's family owned. It was far more than a little vacation cabin. Perhaps it was time to reveal more of the truth to Devyn to help him understand the significance behind their connection and relationship.

Jacob dropped his messenger bag on a nearby chair. Then he went to the fireplace. Since his magic was snow and ice based, he couldn't magic a fire. He needed to do it the old fashion way. Earlier he laid the logs and tinder, he snagged the matchbox. With a practiced flit of his wrist, he struck a couple of matches against the box to light them. Then he held them to the twisted newspaper until they caught flame and tossed the used matches onto the logs.

Turning away from the fireplace, he realized Devyn didn't move from their entrance space. "Icicles," he muttered.

Devyn remained silent.

"Devyn, take off your coat and scarf, hang them on the pegs, go to the sofa with your briefcase, and sit down," he ordered in a somewhat organized list.

Upon the order, Devyn removed the items, hung them in their place, and walked to the sofa. Then he sat down on the leather sofa, kept himself perfectly straight, and placed the briefcase on his lap.

"Snowflakes." Muttering to himself, Jacob went to another room, grabbed a standing mirror, the Talvi Cheval, and brought it back to the main room. He braced it so the glass would face him and Devyn.

"Please be available and not out galivanting somewhere. I don't know who else can help us. I don't trust the other reindeers or know their reputations." Jacob touched a certain set of engraved snowflake and reindeer images. At the same time, he called upon his innate frost magic to activate the link and the Talvi Cheval's power. "I call Strike, Scion of Blitzen, Cheimon Patrol Division — Alaska."

Chapter Two

The glass swirled and the interior image of the Alaskan base of the Cheimon Patrol Division appeared. Sleigh bells jingled multiple times to announce the connection on both sides.

The CPD was the reconnaissance and enforcement team of the North Pole Dimension to maintain the balance of the Naughty & Nice Lists, the very basis of the Dimension's magic and power. Most bases had multiple CPD agents, who were the scions of the original eight reindeer. Some reindeer even maintained their shifting abilities. One of the oldest and strongest reindeer, Strike, commanded Alaska on his own with his brother, Krieg, in charge of the technical stuff. This was who Jacob hoped to connect and help save his connection to Devyn.

"Strike? Krieg? Is anyone there?" Jacob called out.

A young man tilted into view from the left edge. His shaggy reddish-brown hair fell across his face and almost covered his wire-rimmed glasses and light green eyes. He blinked slow before his eyes widened with surprise. "Hello? Oh. Icicles! Sweet snowflakes, this ancient thing works. Don't get many mirror calls. Most prefer cell phones or a Zoom meeting."

"Krieg, hello, yes, the mirror works. It is called the Talvi Cheval. The mirror is always dependable when used properly and doesn't rely on human technology. Electronics are a bit fussy in Frost-created dimensions that split us from human reality timelines," Jacob said.

"Really? Didn't know that part."

"Now you do."

"Good to know. Umm. Sorry." Krieg waved. "Hello. You are—"

"Jacob Serac. I need to speak with Strike. Is he available?"

"Jacob Serac? The chief Frost of the Northeast coast?" Krieg's eyes widened. "Oh, sweet snowflakes, a Frost scion."

"Yeah. Yeah. The high and mighty Jack Frost's kid."

"Not many times removed like the newer Frosts."

Jacob waved away the connection. "Not worth all the hype. Trust me."

Krieg snorted. "Not on our end. You're a legend in most gatherings and stories. A pleasure to meet you."

"Legend? Really?"

"Some even thought you were gone. Like frozen for something."

"No. Still here."

"So, I can see."

Needing to hurry things along, Jacob sighed and asked, "Is Strike available? I need his assistance with a problem."

"Oh, yes, sorry, there would be a reason you called us. Umm... Lemme check." Krieg leaned out of the mirror's image. "Yup. He's in his office. I'll get him."

"Appreciate it."

With a nod, Krieg disappeared from the mirror.

While he waited, Jacob paced a couple of times. "I'm so sorry, Devyn. This isn't what I planned."

Devyn didn't respond or move.

"Hello, Jacob, this is an unexpected call. Especially using a mirror. There were a few times I thought I should move this ancient thing to storage. Good thing I kept it out," a man said when he appeared in the glass. His hair was a glossy reddish brown and his eyes were deep green. He leaned his powerful frame back against the nearest desk. Wearing a soft deep blue hand-knitted sweater, he paired it with dark jeans and heavy boots. A normal person would never realize this man was an ancient reindeer shifter and powerful CPD Field Agent.

"Hello, Strike. Thanks for keeping it around. I wouldn't know how else to reach you except to go through your headquarters."

"Hmm, we'll keep them out of things for now." Strike tilted his head. "Why would I receive an unexpected Talvi Cheval call from a Frost scion? Didn't think the Frosts would have anything to do with the reindeer and the CPD."

"Can we get past the whole reindeer and Frost thing? We're too damn old and seen more than enough to no longer have stars in our eyes and deal with old-fashioned no longer relevant grievances. Earlier generations. Not our problems. Please?"

Strike nodded. "Agreed."

"Grateful. I require your help and expertise to assist with an issue regarding my crystal partner." Jacob looked over his shoulder. "Well, look for yourself to see the issue. It's a little hard to explain without the visual." He stepped to the side to reveal the quiet, motionless Devyn.

"*Hunh*." Strike tilted his head while he studied Devyn. "That's an unusual reaction for a human. Or would this be considered a non-reaction? Especially after all this revelation of magic. He should be hopping up and down and screaming."

"That's a little creepy," Krieg added. With a shudder, he moved back out of sight of the mirror connection.

Jacob glanced at Devyn and back to the mirror. "That would be a normal reaction with someone, yes, but not this case. At least at this moment. I agree that it is quite creepy and disturbing."

"Does he move?" Strike asked.

"Not unless I tell him. And I need to make sure my words are specific or things could go haywire. I'll give you an example." Jacob turned to Devyn. "Devyn, place your briefcase on the floor."

Devyn shifted to set the briefcase in place and returned to his former position.

"Interesting." Strike glanced between them. "Did you give him something?"

"A concoction from the R&D elves in a liquid form placed in a small injector needle. There was holly berry, mistletoe, chamomile, and lavender with a burst of my Frost magic to activate it." Jacob paced a moment while he explained the situation. He pulled out and held up the used needle the elves sent him. "This is the needle. They promised it would stun him, make him compliant for a brief time to get him out of his office and into the elevator. Then I took him through a snow globe portal from the elevator to here."

"This frozen stupor began immediately upon injection. Correct?"

Jacob nodded.

"I've used the concoction myself multiple times to move complicated issues and barriers while after a N&N target. This exact reaction happened three times to me in all this time. The concoction hasn't been changed or altered in decades, at least within in my memory. It's a rare reaction among humans."

"Really? This isn't a new thing."

"It happened when we realized the mortal carried Cheimon genes. They weren't pure mortal."

"Cheimon blood? Devyn?" Jacob stared at Devyn over his shoulder. "I've never seen any possibilities or abilities of Cheimon blood."

"Does he carry your crystal heart?"

"Yes, the crystal is on the tie pin he wears every day. I offered it to him during our first Winter Solstice when we pledged our love."

"No unusual reactions?"

"No, not for the last eight years. He's gotten a little more distant over time which is why I needed to bring him here for the Solstice. I felt a few splinters occur within the heart. There's a darkness around him at times. I believe my crystal heart is cracking due to this increased darkness and distance."

"Falling icicles," Strike muttered the low-end curse. "Krieg, has there been any notifications in the area around Jacob? The Beacon should have pinged on any changes in his crystal partner."

"Checking now." Krieg tapped on the keys. "Nothing."

"Icicles, what is happening with the Beacon?"

"Is there a problem?" Jacob asked.

"Possibly. But not an issue right now." Strike held up a hand. "First, we need to learn if your Devyn has Cheimon blood. Do you have the testing kit?"

"No. Never needed one and don't know how to use it. It's not part of a Frost's collection of gear."

"May I come through a portal? Krieg can lock in on your location through the mirror. I can apply the kit for an accurate read of his genetics. Those answers will narrow down our options to reverse this problem."

"Please. I need this problem answered and fixed before the Solstice ends. If my crystal cracks further or, Frosti forbid, shatters and Devyn's pledge is broken, then I'll disappear into an ice sleep. I don't believe I'll have the time to find someone new to carry my heart."

"And cause damage to your humanity until you either find a new carrier or return from the ice cavern."

"There might not be a chance of returning."

"Icicles. Fifth?"

"Almost. It's different for every scion. I'm one of the oldest and long-lasting. The cavern might order my eternal ice sleep at any shattering. Only the Spirit of Winter can alter the cavern's desires and orders."

"I understand." Strike looked over his shoulder. "Krieg. Connect a portal to Jacob's home. I'll get an ID kit and a couple other things." He disappeared from the mirror.

Krieg reappeared to look around the room. "Let's see where to put one." Then he nodded. "Got it. One portal in the back corner. Looks like a good spot."

"Thank you," Jacob said.

"If I may ask you something while we wait for Strike," Krieg said.

"Go ahead."

"You know there is a CPD base closer. Why did you call us?"

"I trust the history and reputation of Strike out of all the agents."

"He would appreciate the thought and sentiment, of course, but you would never get it from him."

"Another trait I admire."

"Hope Strike can help you and your partner. With so few Frost scions, we need everyone healthy to maintain the winter magic balance."

"Pardon? What do you mean?"

Krieg leaned forward. "Have you heard the updates?"

"Not recently, no. The situation with my partner has occupied most of my attention. What is happening? Is the situation critical?"

"Too many hearts have been shattering. Latest one is Darío Escarcha to slip into an ice sleep."

"Darío? Of the Spanish Frosts? He's around my age and strength."

"That's the worry. If someone of his age could get shattered—" Krieg trailed off with a shrug.

"Then could I be next?"

Krieg nodded.

"What's being done?"

"Not sure. It's a mystery why it's happening because everyone knows how careful a Frost scion is in choosing their partner."

"Did any of the others have a Beacon warning?"

Krieg shook his head. "That's the other concern."

"That's why Strike asked you to check."

"Yes. It's a strange occurrence since Frosts are so connected to the Beacon and the Dimension."

"Is anyone trying to figure out what is happening?"

"Kringle is contacting Spirit of Winter, Mother Nature, and a few other big ones to figure out answers."

"Jokul Frosti? That Spirit of Winter."

"Yes. The only one I know about."

"Oh, sweet icicles, there are lower ones to help the Spirit. But if he went straight to the top one, that's a big step," Jacob said. He blew out a long breath while his mind raced with the news. "Guess Grandpa Jack and his cohorts aren't doing a decent job creating extra scions to replace the ones going into the ice sleep. Or those who are Frosts aren't stepping up to learn about their gifts and taking their positions. Not that I would blame the more modern Frost scions, this isn't always the best life to live."

"Snowflakes, yes. Anyway, thought I would warn you about it since they might call you. Perhaps what Strike learns about your partner could help the others. Might offer up an answer. Or something."

"Appreciate the intel. Thank you."

"Good luck, sir."

"Open the portal, Krieg," Strike called out.

"Back to work," Krieg said and backed out of range. "Opening portal in three... two... one."

Jacob stood and turned when the familiar icy blue swirl appeared in the far corner.

Devyn didn't move.

The six-foot plus tall Strike stepped through the portal. He carried a backpack over one shoulder. The portal closed behind him. "Good evening, Jacob. This is a delightful place you have here."

"Welcome to my island home, Strike. I created a storm to maintain our privacy and contain any magical use from detection," Jacob said. "No one can locate the island on radar or satellite."

"Appreciate it. Makes things a bit easier to cover."

"Plus, I needed the barrier to keep my partner disconnected from his office."

Strike chuckled.

"Problems of having a stubborn, driven mortal of the modern age. Though, he's gotten worse since his promotion to upper management. The problem has increased over the last two years. Which is when I began to feel the issues settle within the crystal that signified there could be trouble between us." Jacob motioned toward Devyn. "This is my chosen crystal partner, Devyn Risher."

Strike moved through the room and studied Devyn. He tilted his head and waved a hand to call up a bit of magic. Then he frowned.

"What is it?"

"There is a bit of darkness surrounding him. Something unusual. Like a flavor of dark ælf, but worse."

"I thought I felt the same back in his office when I first confronted him to come with me. What does this shadow mean?"

"I'm not sure. Let me first test what is happening with Devyn. Then we'll figure out the other part of the problem."

"Which expanded into something beyond a simple allergic reaction."

"Possibly." Strike pulled a chair closer to where Devyn sat on the sofa. He set the backpack on the table. Then he went through a series of simple movements to evaluate Devyn's reactions and responses.

Jacob could only stand and watch while the CPD agent performed the assessment. He ached with the idea he caused Devyn pain. He wanted to discuss their problems and his concerns and figure out how to fix the cracks. Though part of the withdrawal could be all the falsehoods Jacob had to use to protect his true identity. If Devyn was Cheimon, then he could explain more to him. "Is it the same as the other ones who had this strange paralysis?"

"Yes, almost the exact same reactions to those with the Cheimon blood," Strike said. "This particular concoction is made for pure humans. Cheimon blood requires a different mixture." He opened the backpack and removed a kit. "Can you roll up his left sleeve? I need to wrap this ID band around his forearm, close to the elbow."

"Devyn, hold out your left arm," Jacob said while he sat on the coffee table.

Devyn did as commanded.

"Can all this be reversed?" Jacob unbuttoned the cuff and rolled up the sleeve to the desired location.

"If it's the same reaction as the others, then, yes, there is a reversal. He would need to drink polar snow and eternal snowflakes mixed with your magic. It'll remove the potion from his system. Since your magic activated the potion, you would essentially deactivate it."

"Just a zap of my magic wouldn't help?"

"Nope. The snow mixture will remove any traces of the potion from his bloodstream and allow it to pass through his normal bodily functions." Strike removed a fresh ID band from the packaging and wrapped it around Devyn's forearm. He pressed a button to activate the band.

Jacob watched the blue lights appear on the band's surface while the tiny ID machine worked to gather Devyn's blood and analyze the genetic patterns.

The band beeped for Strike to remove it. Then Strike inserted one end into a small glass machine and pressed a few more buttons. A piece of paper printed from the bottom.

Strike removed the paper and read the results aloud. "Cheimon."

"What? No way."

"Forty-two percent. A mixture of Christmas Elf and Dark Ælf. The rest is plain mortal from a Scottish and Norwegian bloodline which could explain his blond hair and blue eyes."

"Are you kidding me?"

Strike shook his head. He handed over the paper.

"Unbelievable." Jacob took it to double-check the findings, but he knew there wasn't a chance of a false positive. Not with the R&D creations. Those industrious elves did everything possible to make sure all their gadgets and machines worked with perfection and accuracy for every agent in the field. The magical potions had some variations and issues. Like the current reaction Devyn experienced.

"Your partner's Cheimon and can enter the Dimension. He's over the twenty-five percent limitation. Perhaps his abilities aren't active or responsive. Many new Cheimon scions of elf, pixie, fairy, Frost, and even reindeer don't have any knowledge or abilities unless something activates them. It's frustrating and a bit scary at how the bloodlines thinned and became forgotten among the generations."

Jacob touched Devyn's cheek. "What does this mean for our crystal partnership? Would it alter anything?"

"Your crystal would be far more reactive to anyone with the Cheimon blood because our lines are interconnected with the Pole. Could be why you were able to sense the smallest of cracks and changes within your crystal. Overall, it would be more beneficial for you to remain with him. That is if it's possible to maintain your relationship and the crystal's strength. There's enough Cheimon to increase his lifespan, but the longevity connection within the crystal would extend him further without any harm."

"Then it's not going to hurt him."

"Not that I know, but I don't know all the history about a Frost scion with a Cheimon partner. Don't know if there's any research about the connection. Best to speak with the library elves in the Dimension, they have the ancient scrolls and books to do the required research. Given time, I expect some Cheimon gifts to appear with the deepening connection to your magic and the crystal. Especially if you visit the Dimension with him." Strike removed another box from the backpack. "Do you have a drinking glass and spoon?"

"Yes. Give me a moment," Jacob said and left the room. Within moments, he returned with a small glass and spoon and set them on the table. He sat on the sofa next to Devyn.

"Appreciate it." Strike poured pure Pole snow from a vial. Then he added a pinch of eternal snowflakes he gathered from a small pouch. He mixed them with the spoon and handed the glass to Jacob. "Add your magic. The snow will melt with your magic. Then ask him to drink it. He should snap right out of it, but he'll be a bit disoriented while he resets."

Jacob glanced at the mixture. "Okay. Thank you." He charged the glass's contents with his magic and watched the snow glow and melt. He placed it in Devyn's hand. "Devyn, I need you to drink this." He sat on the coffee table to watch.

Without a word, Devyn drank the contents. He set the glass down on the table.

"I hope this works," Jacob said.

"Same here. You never know how some could react to anything. When he snaps out of it, we'll figure out the other half of your problem." Strike gathered both kits and returned them to the backpack. "I'll add Devyn's information to the database. Could you let me know the results after this Solstice for the records?"

"I will. If I'm still around and not in an ice coma."

Devyn belched deep and meaty.

"That means it's working," Strike said.

Devyn belched again. Then a fart ripped out.

They tried not to crack up laughing while they waited. Even immortal, gas humor never got old.

Chapter Three

About ten to fifteen minutes later, Devyn blinked his eyes and shook his head. He pressed his fingers against the bridge of his nose and groaned. "What happened? I have such a headache."

"Side effect," Strike muttered to Jacob.

Blinking again, Devyn looked up, moved his gaze from Jacob to Strike, and back multiple times. Then he looked around the room. He returned his stare back to Jacob and raised an eyebrow. "What happened? Who is this? Where are we? Is this the cabin? How did we get here? I was in Boston."

"Umm." Jacob winced at the rapid-fire questions. Then he wiggled in his spot on the coffee table. "Yeah, the situation kind of gotten screwed up and I had to adjust things. My plan didn't quite work out as planned, but we're in my cabin. The one we visit every Winter Solstice."

"I couldn't join you this year. I'm busy with the Tokyo project. I thought I explained all that to you. I need to be in Boston, Jacob."

"Yeah. I know."

"Damn it, Jacob, I could lose my job because of this!" Devyn pushed to his feet, wobbled, and dropped back down. A belch left him. "Whoa—" His hand went back to hold his head and rub his temples. "Ow... My head."

"Devyn—"

Devyn held up his free hand. Then he pointed a finger at Strike. "Who are you? How do you fit in all of this mess?"

"My name is Strike. I'm an old friend and work acquaintance of Jacob's. He asked me for some help with you," Strike said.

"Strike? Just Strike? Like Madonna or Sting?"

The ancient reindeer shifter nodded his head. "Though I don't have a decent singing voice, but yes."

"Fine. Whatever." Devyn glared at Jacob. "What is happening to me? What did you do to me? I need to be in Boston."

"You had an odd reaction to something Jacob gave you," Strike answered him instead of Jacob. "I helped figure out what was happening, but I think there's something else going on with you."

"Like what?" Devyn asked. "What did you give me?"

"Something to help bring you out of Boston," Jacob said. "It didn't happen like I planned."

"Shit. No, I guess it didn't." Devyn narrowed his gaze. "What would drive you do to this to me?"

"The crystal is splintering," Jacob said.

"What?"

Jacob leaned over to release the tie pin from Devyn's semi-perfect knotted tie. He plucked the small crystal from the housing. Then with his magic, he enlarged it to the full heart-sized crystal. There were significant cracks and shadows throughout the crystalline heart. It was worse than Jacob thought. He cradled the heart between his hands. "Do you remember when I offered this to you?"

Devyn pulled back and stared at the crystal. "It didn't look like that."

"No. It's supposed to be clear and solid, like a perfect diamond. This is the damage done over the last two years. You pulled away from me since your promotion. Every time you pulled away, ignored me, and snubbed our relationship for your work or something else that came between us, another splinter or crack happened."

"What about those dark spots?"

"I never saw them before and don't know how they occur. It's rather distressing and unsettling to see what happened." Jacob glanced to Strike. "Any ideas?"

"I might have one, but I need some information." Strike leaned forward and asked, "Devyn, did anything odd happen during your promotion? Were you given something personal to keep with you at all times, perhaps to wear or touch it?"

"What? I don't understand. I got a new office and a parking spot like all upper management. Then a shit load of work got dumped on my spiffy new desk for me to figure out," Devyn said.

"Think back. Perhaps it is something personal. It could be a gift from someone on the board or another member of management. Is there anything that jogs your memory?"

Devyn yanked his tie loose and removed it. Then when he went to remove his jacket, he stopped while his hand hovered around his chest. "No way. Really? Could that—" He slipped his hand into an inner pocket and brought out a gold pocket watch. "One of the board members gave this to me as a welcome to the management gift. He mentioned everyone received a watch upon their promotion."

"Have you kept it on you every day since the promotion?"

"Well, yes, I would seem stupid to not wear it."

"Can you describe him to me? Know his name?"

"Victor Merrowynd." Devyn continued with the description of the older executive.

Strike glanced at Jacob and back to Devyn. "Merrowynd?" He spelled the unusual last name.

Devyn nodded while he twirled the watch between his fingers. "That's him. The Third or Fourth. His family is one of the original founders of the company."

"Do you know the name?" Jacob asked Strike, but figured he would know the answer. It wasn't a good one.

The ancient reindeer glanced over and lifted an eyebrow.

"Icicles," Jacob cursed. "Did not want to see that." He grumbled. "You're not thinking that this relates back to the Yule Lads and Grýla."

"Who else could it be?"

"Icicles…"

The reindeer didn't respond while he jotted notes on a thin glass pad with a stylus.

"What is that? How does that work?" The engineer brain inside Devyn became curious when Strike used the glass pad.

"Sorry. Proprietary information," Strike said.

"Come on. Really?"

Strike nodded.

"Fine. Whatever. Since you won't tell me about the pad, then there's nothing else. Because, as usual, I have no idea what you two were talking about. Yule Lads? What next? So… Can we get back to my watch?" Before Jacob could press for details, Devyn held out the watch. "It's a beautiful piece of artisanship. Keeps perfect time and date. You can even see the intricate gears through a glass panel."

An aura of darkness overwhelmed Jacob and ground against his pure winter magic and light. He grimaced and leaned back. "Yeah, icicles, that is giving me a headache." He placed his fingers to his forehead. "I would say that's the cause of all the problems. The darkness must have been masked by his jackets' linings which are usually silk."

"I agree. This is definitely a problem and a deliberate placement," Strike said after he scowled and shook his head. "Wow. That is some powerful mojo."

"What is wrong with both of you? There's nothing wrong with my watch. Look, it's even engraved." Devyn hit the button to pop open the designed top to reveal the beautiful mother-of-pearl face, inner workings, and the inner side engraved interior with Devyn's name, the company, and the date of his promotion.

Both Pole men grimaced even harder at the dark aura's power.

Strike reached into his bag and pulled out a folded silk handkerchief. He shook it out, laid it on the table, and scooted around to give them room. "Please place the watch on the silk."

"What? Why? Are you going to destroy it? You are. Aren't you?"

"I'm not going to destroy it. I promise, but neither of us can touch it. There's something dark surrounding that watch and it's dangerous to us," Strike said. "It's also changing you to cause the effect on the crystal. Either way, we must remove the shadow."

"Is this something about that magic stuff?" Devyn asked Jacob.

"Magic stuff?" Jacob's jaw dropped. "Are you kidding me? Is that what you think I am? What I do?" His fingers clutched the delicate heart. "Do you think this heart is a stupid prop? A piece of glass?"

Devyn shrugged.

"Calm down, Frost. It's the influence of the dark aura," Strike said.

"But—"

"Let's banish the aura first. Then concentrate on your ego and relationship."

Jacob brushed his fingers across the delicate, fragile heart. "The shadows in the crystal—"

"Could be from the influence of the watch's aura. You didn't feel any issues until the timing when he received the watch," Strike finished. "That's what I'm thinking."

"Can it be removed?"

"We'll find out. Please, Devyn, place the watch on the silk." Strike motioned to the handkerchief. Then he pulled out the pouch of snowflakes and a miniature empty snow globe from his backpack.

"There better be no damage to this watch. It was a gift," Devyn said while he placed the watch on the silk and stretched out the golden chain.

"A gift laced with a dark aura," Strike said.

"Which could mean what?" Jacob asked.

"Someone knew he was connected to you, Jacob," Strike said.

"I don't believe either of you. This could all be some fluke and farce to fuck around with me," Devyn said. "I wouldn't put it past you messing around with me, Jacob, not after all the crap."

"Crap? What crap?" Jacob asked Devyn.

"Not now, Jacob. Let me concentrate on manipulating this bit of nastiness in some measure of peace. Please? I really don't want it to lash out at any one of us," Strike admonished them. He sprinkled some eternal snowflakes across the watch with a whisper of his power and some words.

A wisp of dark smoke lifted from the watch.

"Sweet snowflakes," Jacob whispered.

"What the hell is that?" Devyn asked.

"Definitely a dark magic spell. A touch of Dark Ælf, but something more. Something from nasty side of the Dimension." Strike glanced at Jacob. "Definitely from one of the Yule Lads, if not their mother. This is dangerous." He picked up the empty globe. "Jacob, open the mirror connection. Get Krieg on the line. I need to get this spell into isolation and inspection. Fast."

"Open the mirror connection? What are you talking about?" Devyn asked.

Jacob stood, kept the heart in one hand, and walked to the mirror. He touched the engraved snowflake and reindeer image. At the same time, he called upon his innate Frost magic to activate the link. "I call Krieg, Scion of Blitzen, Cheimon Patrol Division — Alaska."

The mirror swirled once more to reveal the Alaska office. Jingle bells rang when the connection finished.

"Holy crap! What is that?" Devyn asked.

The younger reindeer technician leaned into view. He adjusted his wire-rimmed glasses. "Umm. Hello? Two calls in one day. Wow. What's happening? Oh, hey, the stoned dude is awake. Hey there." He waved a hand along with a bright smile.

"Stoned dude?" Devyn asked. "Who the hell are you?"

"Umm— Krieg. Hi. Techno geek," Krieg said with a grin and another wave. Then he checked the two immortals. "I think I'm missing something—"

"Krieg, need a small portal next to me. ASAP," Strike called out. "Powerful dark mist spell coming through in a globe. Immediate Level Five isolation and transfer to R&D for a full analysis under the strictest controls."

"Sweet icicles! A Five?"

"Potential Yule Lads issue. Open it."

"Got it!" Krieg said.

Jacob turned to watch Strike work.

Strike held the globe over the watch. He spun it carefully under a fall of snowflakes and magic to draw the vapor into the globe. When he contained the wisp, he sealed the globe with a smear of snowflakes and magic. "Now, Krieg!"

A small blue portal swirled out of nowhere next to Strike.

"What the hell is that!" Devyn shouted.

Strike tossed the globe through the portal.

In the mirror, Krieg captured the globe inside a clear box. He dropped the lid and used a heat gun that squirted out melted evergreen tree sap to create a seal. Then he placed the small box into a second larger box and repeated the sealing process. "Any further information?"

"Dark aura spell located on a gold watch given to the Cheimon-mortal partner of a Frost scion, Jacob Serac, in a specific and deliberate fashion. Name of possible perpetrator is Victor Merrowynd. Connection to Dark Pole, the Yule Lads, and Grýla. Find out which Lad he belongs too. Spell caused distance between them along with shadows and cracks in the crystal heart. Known two-year timeframe upon receipt of watch," Strike said in a succinct matter-of-fact report tone.

"Icicles. Now the Merrowynd. We dealt with one of their nasty tricks in Canada. The blasted Lads slipped out of every trap and battle without a spot on their precious high-powered suits," Krieg muttered while he tapped away and sent the box through a different portal.

"Who is in charge of the Northeast CPD office?"

"Dasher's line is in charge. There's been some trouble though. A change of the top agent and a few other problems."

"Who's in charge? Where is it?"

"Asher. The office is located outside of Boston."

"That'll be my next stop. Give them a warning. I'll create my own portal."

"Will do." Krieg signed off.

"CPD office? We live across the bay from downtown Boston," Jacob said.

"There should have been a blip on the N&N list regarding Devyn's slide into the darkness. Especially since he's connected to you."

"I remember you asked Krieg to check the Beacon."

"That's right. There should have been an alert. Someone should have figured out what was happening within a couple of months of Devyn receiving this gift. That's the longest amount of time I would give it to make sure there was something truly going wrong. The office should have alerted you to help figure out the problem, long before you felt the cracks. I'm going to figure out what in Blitzen's lightning is happening over there," Strike said. "I don't like it when an office fails in their duties."

"Krieg mentioned about the other hearts shattering."

"It could all be relevant. Either way, I need to figure out what in icicles is happening with the Beacon and the list."

"Going to kick some butt?" Jacob asked.

"Dark ice, right. There's no excuse to let a blip linger. No matter how busy an office is," Strike said.

"What the hell is going on around here?" Devyn demanded.

Strike and Jacob turned to look at the third man in the room.

"Residuals of the dark spell should disappear within the next few hours. Perhaps, then, you two should take some time to talk about what is happening between you and the meaning behind his bloodwork," Strike said.

"Talk about what? Bloodwork? What bloodwork?" Devyn looked to Jacob.

"There's a lot we need to discuss, Devyn. But not quite yet, like Strike mentioned—"

"Oh, come on, Jacob!"

"Please listen. You remain under the spell's influence and don't have a clear head. You might not understand what I'm explaining or twist it about without even knowing what you're doing," Jacob said.

"Then you'll tell me the truth. All of it. Don't hold back on anything," Devyn said.

Jacob nodded.

"Perhaps a visit to the homeland might be required to help with the explanations and make things stick. In a fashion," Strike said. "Always good to have a full visual instead of words. Especially when it deals with the NPD."

"NPD?" Devyn asked.

Jacob looked at him.

"Okay. Okay." Devyn threw up his hands.

"Good idea, Strike, thanks," Jacob said.

The reindeer shrugged. "Got a travel snow globe?"

"Yes, I stocked up on a few things."

With a nod, Strike pulled out a clear snow globe from his backpack. He closed the backpack and slung the strap over his shoulder while he rose to his feet. "I hope everything works out between you two. It was a pleasure to finally meet and speak with you, Jacob. Call again anytime." He wandered back to the far back corner of the main room.

"Thank you again. For everything."

"CPD Northeast office. Boston. Asher, Scion of Dasher," Strike spoke to the globe along with a burst of his power. He tossed it into the corner.

An icy blue portal appeared.

"Whoa!" Devyn said.

Strike glanced over his shoulder and smiled. "It's a nifty trick. You'll learn about this and more, Devyn. Good to meet you, take care of our Frost. We need to keep him out of the ice."

"What?" Devyn asked.

With a chuckle, Strike waved away his comment. "You'll learn. Promise." He glanced back to Jacob. "I'll get the Boston office straightened and have them figure out who this Merrowynd board member is and how he connected Devyn to you. Could be a member of the dark side of the Pole. Not looking forward to that answer, but I'll get it figure out. If it turns out to be the Yules, be careful of a counter offense when they realize their spell is broken. Anything could happen with them from mischief to murder."

"Understood. Thanks for the warning. Not my first time dealing with one of the Lads or even their ogress mother. Thank you, Strike, I appreciate you coming," Jacob said.

"Thanks for calling me. Anytime you need something, give me a call. Frost and CPD should work together more often."

"Don't know why we're not more interconnected."

"I'll make a note of it when I speak with Kringle and the Pole Council." With a nod and smile, Strike stepped through the portal and disappeared.

Chapter Four

When the portal disappeared in a burst of sparkles after Strike went through, Jacob turned to face Devyn. "Well…"

"Well? Sheesh, Jacob!" Devyn rubbed his hands over his face. "I feel so damn lost. What the hell is happening today? I don't understand anything about you, us, or what happened with that guy."

"I didn't mean for things to happen this way, but I'm desperate to reach you. You kept pulling away and avoiding me. I felt I had no other way, but to bring you here to the cabin. I had no idea you would react bad to the potion and there was a dark spell," Jacob said while he sat down on the coffee table to face Devyn. "Please, forgive me, Devyn."

Devyn glanced at the crystal Jacob placed on a blue silk cushion. "It's all about the crystal. That is all you care about."

"No, Devyn, there's much more to us than the crystal. It's a manifestation and physical personification of my heart, power, and love for you. Without you, I'm lost to my magic and the ice. You keep me alive."

"I don't think I understood what you meant when you first handed me the pin. Let alone believe anything you told me about your past. I never could figure out how to tell you."

Jacob nodded. "I didn't know how much I could explain. There's been some issues with revealing everything."

"How?"

"Last time I tried to say everything, my chosen crystal bearer became quite insane. He couldn't understand and accept the truth behind the myths. He never met Strike or anyone else from the Pole. I decided that I wouldn't give him my crystal. Then I walked away so

I could find another connection. I ended up finding you. Only, now things are in trouble between us and I'm a bit scared."

"That's not good."

Jacob shook his head.

"Give me some time. Okay? I have a wicked headache and dizzy from whatever you two did to me."

"I apologize for you being unwell. An unexpected side effect from what happened." Jacob leaned back against the sofa's side. "I packed a suitcase for you for the weekend. It's in the master bedroom. The upstairs loft." He waved a hand toward the stairs. "Take a shower, change into something comfortable, and take a nap. You need the rest. I'll have something ready to eat by the time you wake up. We can talk tomorrow with clearer heads."

"You don't mind waiting that long."

"I'm considered immortal among the Frosts. I've been alive an exceptionally long time, even in between my ice sleep. I can wait a few hours for you to take a nap and decide what you want to do. It's entirely in your hands if you wish to keep my crystal heart or walk away from everything. I can't force your decision, only explain things to help aid you in figuring out what you wish to do," Jacob said.

"Immortal? Ice sleep?"

Rising to his feet, Jacob shrugged. "All part of the explanations."

"Hmm. Sneaky bugger."

Jacob chuckled. "That's how it works."

Devyn rose to his feet and glanced at the briefcase. "Will any of that work here?"

"Not this weekend. Mia is taking care of everything at the office this weekend. I blocked things for a while, so we're not distracted."

"I'll leave it upstairs with my suitcase. Keep it out of sight," Devyn said while he grabbed the handle. "What about the watch? My pin..."

"Let's make sure the spell is completely gone and it doesn't rebound. It's safe where it is. I'll keep the pin here on the table with the crystal."

"Until all of this is settled—"

"And a decision is made," Jacob finished. Then he nodded. "Yes."

"Okay," Devyn said and headed for the single staircase. He paused and looked down at Jacob. "Thank you, Jacob." Without waiting for a response, he disappeared around the corner.

Jacob watched him disappear around the stairs. He let out a long sigh and hoped things would be a bit smoother for the rest of the weekend.

Remembering Strike's idea of a trip to the Pole, he went to a box on top of a cabinet, slid his finger along the edge to unlock it, and pulled out a small glass tablet created by the R&D elves to be a communicator. He tapped out a code on the screen and pulsed his power.

"Mistletoe Jangle," he spoke to the glass to place the call.

"Season's greetings. This is the Pole home of Frost scion, Jacob Serac. Mistletoe speaking," a bright, cheery voice said through the glass.

"Mistle, it's Jacob. How are you doing today?" he asked his Pole house elf.

"Season's greetings, Mister Jacob! A pleasure to hear from you. Sweet snow, all is going well. Like always. A cheery, blustery day in the Dimension," the elf said. "How are things with your crystal chosen?"

"There's been a few developments. Devyn is part-Cheimon. Someone covered him in a dark spell. My crystal heart is shadowed with a few cracks."

"Oh, gingersnap cookies, how did all this happen?"

"I'm not sure. I called upon Strike to help. He helped undo the potion's side effect and remove the spell. He also performed the blood test. We believe the spell could be from the Lads, but it is under investigation. Though, please keep things on high alert for anything that changes. If it were the Lads, they could retaliate anywhere when they realized we figured out their plans."

"Sweet snow! I will inform the Nutcracker captain and toy soldiers in the area, Mister Jacob, for the protection. The Lads got to your chosen. How?"

"That's what Strike is trying to figure out. He suggested I bring Devyn to the Pole to help explain everything."

"Sweet snow! A Cheimon crystal chosen. How strange? Gingersnaps, I need to clean. Everything."

Jacob chuckled. "I'm sure the house is sparkling clean under your care and attention, Mistle. I wanted to alert you to our visit. I'll call before we use the globe."

"Of course, Mister Jacob. I will do my utmost to ensure a perfect visit for your chosen. We will get your heart fixed in a gingersnap jiffy. Can't have you slipping into an ice sleep. Too much to do to allow that to happen. Not on Mistletoe's watch." With that, the house elf hung up after a cheery farewell.

Jacob placed the tablet back into the box along with other Pole items. He flicked his finger along the hidden lock to engage it.

Then he went to the kitchen to figure out what to make for dinner.

* * * *

HOURS LATER, HE HAD created a decent winter stew and fresh bread with a bit of extra magical help to speed things along. Deciding to spruce things up a bit more, Jacob spread out a pale blue tablecloth and smoothed out the wrinkles. Then he picked out the nicer bowls, silverware, cloth napkins, and glasses. He laid out everything to create a special table for two. A pair of silver candlesticks and smaller votives added a bit more flickers of light. As an extra touch, he clipped a few evergreen branches from a nearby tree to add ambience and a natural fragrance to enhance the experience.

"Something smells delicious."

At the soft words, Jacob spun to watch Devyn move down the stairs in a graceful fashion. His hair stuck up in bed-mussed spikes, but it was becoming for him. He changed into comfortable fleece pants, a T-shirt, and tugged on a deep green cardigan his mother knitted years ago. In deference to the cold floors, he slipped on a pair of wool-lined loafers.

"Hope it tastes just as good. How was your nap?"

"Peaceful and refreshing. I haven't slept that deep in a while." Devyn rubbed the back of his neck.

"And the headache and discomfort?"

"Both are gone. Guess whatever was on the watch did a number on me for a long time." Devyn moved through the room and stopped to stare down at the watch they both left on the coffee table on the silk handkerchief. "Don't know if I even want that thing around me."

"It wasn't the watch that caused the trouble, but the spell attached to it. Strike removed it, as you saw, and rendered the watch back to normal. Just a simple pocket watch." Jacob studied Devyn's movements and behavior. "Don't think we'll understand how the spell truly altered things for you and us. How about we start things at a neutral place?"

"How?"

"Have dinner with me?" Jacob moved back and waved a hand toward the set-up table.

Devyn let out a low whistle. "Nice set-up."

"Wanted to pull out the best. Hungry?"

"Starving."

"Good. I made more than enough." Jacob pulled back a chair for Devyn to sit. "I have water, wine, tea, and apple cider. What would you like?"

"Some iced tea." Devyn settled down in the chair. "I don't want to fuzz my mind again."

"Understood. Feel the same myself," Jacob said while he went to the fridge and pulled out a jug of fresh brewed iced tea and set it on the table. Then he went to the stove and ladled generous helpings of the stew in two bowls. He tossed the rolls into a towel-covered basket and added them to the table. Then he brought over the full steaming bowls. "Careful. It's still hot."

Devyn sniffed at his bowl and hummed in response. "Smells delicious. Along with the bread. What is this soup called?"

"Just a simple winter stew with beef cubes, different winter vegetables, a tomato-based broth, and herbs and spices. I added in some barley to thicken it up. An old family recipe."

"Is it something you pulled together over the years?"

"Bit of this. Bit of that. Tried some herbs. Tried some spices. Also depends on what vegetables are available."

"You went shopping for all of this and more, packed clothes for both of us, and did whatever else you needed to get this place ready without knowing if I would even join you. It's a lot of work," Devyn said while he spooned up some stew, blew on it, and sipped it.

"It's why I used the concoction in the needle to get you moving. Just didn't know about the adverse effects. Please, I do apologize for my decisions in all that happened," Jacob said between spoonful of the stew. He snagged one of the rolls, ripped it, and dipped one end to soak up the broth. "Needs a bit more salt." After munching on the bread, he rose and located the container of Kosher salt he preferred while cooking. He brought it to the table, sprinkled a few granules, and stirred it together. Then with another spoonful, he assessed it and nodded. "Better. Want some?"

"Hmm. Just a bit. Otherwise it's tasty," Devyn said while he pinched a few granules to add to his bowl.

"Here's the rolls."

"Thanks." Devyn grabbed a pair of rolls and set them near his bowl. "How did you get me out of the office?"

"You walked out with me."

"Under the spell."

"Well, yes, surprised your assistant. Mia didn't quite believe that I could get you out, let alone without a word from you. Then we took the quick way out."

"How?"

"One of those globe gates. In the elevator."

"Umm—"

"I frosted over the cameras. No one saw anything. Not my first-time avoiding security cameras."

"Evading the law?" Setting aside the spoon, Devyn ripped a roll in similar style to Jacob and dipped a piece into the bowl. He slipped the covered piece into his mouth and chewed. "Hmm. Yum."

"Bending it a tad," Jacob said with a grin.

Devyn wiggled the spoon at Jacob. "You're hiding something from me."

"Oh, I'm probably hiding a lot."

"Start somewhere—"

Jacob tilted his head. "You don't want to wait."

Devyn shook his head. "Start off easy.

"How old do you think I am?"

"Early forties. There are shades of silver in your white gold hair. A few lines around your eyes and mouth. Your manners and responses," Devyn said. He grinned. "Am I close?"

"Add a few more zeroes."

"What? How many?"

"Let me put it this way. My first adult years were spent marching through battles with Constantine sometime in the fourth century. After my second crystal heart shattered, I woke in the eighth century and watched Charlemagne become crowned king by Pope Leo III. Throughout the centuries, I've fought in the wars, too many to count or remember."

"Whoa!" Devyn's fork hovered over the bowl. "That was—"

"Around 800. If my memory is correct. I was one of the knights in the crowd. Not a major player. Due to my background and purpose in life, I couldn't influence history or draw attention to myself."

"Are you immortal?"

"Close to it."

"Is this why you're more aero or ace than..." Devyn shrugged. "Sexual. Not that it bothers me. I swear. I don't mind the non-sexual aspect."

"Are you sure about that? Since you're bringing it up."

Devyn sighed and set the spoon down. He leaned forward and placed his hand across Jacob's arm. "You know I don't mind that aspect. I'm not all that sexual myself. Is it because of how long you have been around? No longer needing that part of a relationship. I bet you did it all, saw it all, and not much surprises you."

"The sexuality of humans is endless and exponential in the possibilities. Over the centuries, I learned the emotional connection is stronger than anything physical. I don't mind it, occasionally—" Jacob paused and smiled. He glanced at Devyn and wiggled his spoon. "Neither did you."

Devyn grinned. "That one night with the whip cream was... memorable."

Jacob chuckled. "Thought you would bring that one up. Curling up with you on the couch, mugs of hot cocoa nearby, and a couple of movies are my favorite moments. The ones I remember and cherish far more than any sexual encounter."

"Same here." Devyn squeezed Jacob's arm. Then he picked up the spoon and dug back into the bowl. "Back to you being immortal."

"Well. Not quite immortal. There's no exact name for what we are."

"We?"

"Frosts. A collective name for us. We are scions of Jokul Frosti, the Spirit of Winter and father to Jack Frost. They are our father and grandfather several times removed along the bloodline. I'm a direct line descendant of both immortals. Jack Frost is my father, though my mother believed it was her husband who fathered me. The Jacks have a way of disguising themselves to blend in and seduce the ladies."

"Of Jack Frost? The little winter sprite guy in fairy tales?"

"The fairy tales are twists on reality to protect the Cheimon. Jack really hated that part of the tales and what it did to him. At least the Jack I know. There are eight different Jack Frosts spread throughout the world, but they all have the same position within the Frosts."

"What exactly are the Cheimon?"

"That's the name of the bloodlines of the North Pole Dimension."

"The North Pole Dimension?"

"The physical pole is the anchor of another dimension created by the first Santa, Ded Moroz, along with Jokul Frosti and Mother Nature to protect those with the bloodline to live and work. Mortals were becoming far too curious, even more so with various space and ground technology. It covers the entire Artic Circle, which is the boundary line, between the mortal and the NP Dimension. There's an invisible barrier that if someone crosses it, the barrier will determine their bloodline. If a scion of the Dimension, they will enter it. If not, they will remain within the mortal realm."

"Holy sheee-iiiit," Devyn drawled out. Then he got a boyish look on his face. A wide glee-filled smile curled his lips. "Reindeer?"

"Always about the reindeer," Jacob said with a chuckle.

"Classic part of the songs and stories."

"True. Can't get away from them. Not that any of the reindeer genuinely appreciate the song or the tales."

"So they do exist!"

Jacob smiled. "The original eight plus Rudolph all existed. They were shifters which explains how small they appeared in most tales. It's this whole mass dimension transfer that I never could understand. You met two scions of one of the original eight."

"What? No way." Devyn pointed his thumb over his shoulder. "That guy... Strike?"

"And his younger brother, Krieg, in the mirror."

"What line are they from?"

"Blitzen's bloodline descendants."

"That is too crazy." Devyn shook his head. "Strike mentioned I was Cheimon. How is that possible?"

"Some of your ancestors were from the North Pole Dimension. It's the reason behind your reaction to the concoction. He assessed your blood with a specialized kit that analyzed your genetics. Thanks to those ancestors, from multiple lines, you are part Cheimon and can travel to the Dimension."

"But I don't have anything special about me."

"Most do not have any gifts or physical resemblance until some genes are activated or everything remains inert, but the bloodline flows true. No matter how distant or generations removed. Strike will enter your genetic information into our database, perhaps he might find some distant relatives."

"Ones I could actually meet?"

"If they're in the NPD, yes, or around the area we could travel to meet them. I don't see a problem doing that if it's something you desire."

Devyn's jaw dropped. He tapped his spoon against the bowl a couple of times while he tried to figure out what Jacob was telling him. "This is mind-blowing."

"Perhaps too much for one conversation."

"Agreed."

"Want some more stew?" Jacob rose to his feet and pointed to Devyn's bowl.

"Damn. Didn't realize I finished it. Guess I was hungrier than I thought. Yes, please, again, it's delicious," Devyn said and held out the bowl.

"Happy to hear it. I'll make it again." Jacob carried the bowls back to the stove for the refills.

Chapter Five

The hair on the back of his neck rose. Snowflakes swirled within his eyes.

Something or someone activated his outer wards.

It wasn't a friendly poke.

Pissed off someone ventured into his territory without his permission, Jacob dropped the bowls on the counter. He raised his power and built a thick wall of snow and ice around the perimeter to push back the intruders.

"Umm. Jacob? Your skin is blue. Your hair is white. And there's snow falling. Inside," Devyn said.

Jacob shook his head to stop Devyn from talking while he felt along the exterior to figure out what was happening. This was one of those times he wished he installed exterior cameras. Though the fluctuation of magic and energy played all kinds of nasty tricks on technology. Then he felt another release of energy firing against the exterior. "Hit the ice! Now."

"Excuse me? What?"

"I need you to trust and listen to me." Jacob snarled at Devyn. "Drop to the floor and cover your head. Now!"

"What the hell, man? What are you—"

Shadow dark bullets whizzed right past Devyn's nose.

Devyn's eyes widened while his eyebrows lifted. "Holy shit! What was that?"

Another volley of something shot past them. While a different crossfire ricocheted through the entire house.

"Drop! Now!" Jacob raised one hand above his head. With a burst of different energy, he shot his power straight up to send out a desperate call for assistance. The beacon should pulse with the frantic energy he poured into it. Then it should reach all the local Flakes, Verglas, Ice elves and fairies to travel by globe to his cabin now. There's no way he could fight the intruders and protect Devyn. When more bullets whizzed through another layer of his walls, he knew he couldn't counteract this type of shadow magic.

Finally, to his relief, Devyn dropped to the ground underneath the table. He huddled there and wrapped his arms over his head.

Another barrage filled the house. They flickered with magic to flash through walls and windows.

"Why am I not hearing anything get broken?" Devyn asked. "What are those things?"

"Dark magic powers them. They're searching for flesh and ignore anything else. Since they are mostly shadows, they pass through all other targets."

"Why are they doing this?"

Jacob lifted an eyebrow. "Who's the only mortal here? That had a dark magic spell-covered watch and connected to the oldest Frost."

"What? Me? Why me?"

"How should I know? No one knows how to find my island unless I invite them. No one."

"I didn't tell anyone. I have no clue how to get here without you."

Jacob leaned to the side when more shadow needles flashed through the room. He managed to snatch and pinch one from the flight. When he brought it closer, he sniffed, flashed his magic across it for a response, and grumbled under his breath when he got one. "Icicles! Dark magic. Yule Lads. Should have known they would set up an ambush. How did they find us?" He covered the entire needle in a protective layer of frost to contain the integrity and contents of the device. Then he pocketed the needle to hand it over to the CPD. R&D would definitely need to take a look at that dangerous thing and figure out some way to counteract them.

"How did you—"

"Hold up. I need to figure out what to do."

"Oh, right, sure. Cause I'm the dumb mortal who doesn't know shit."

"At this moment, yes, you're the only mortal here who doesn't understand what's at stake if something hits you. I could lose you to whatever is inside those needles. Only this time, there could be no bringing you back from the precipice. Dark magic bullets and needles geared for a mortal are flying through the house, but they're phasing through walls. Do you understand what's at stake? What do you think you can do about it?"

"Umm..."

"Right. Thank you. Now let me think. Icicles, where is the help I summoned?" Either way, he needed to figure out a plan to get out. It appears the best option would be to travel to the NPD. It would be the safest place to keep Devyn until he figured out who gave him the watch and Strike finished his investigation.

Another volley of bullets and needles flew through the house.

As if on cue, five FVI members stepped out of different globe portals.

"Greetings, Lord Frost—" the highest-ranking elf said. A barrage of dark missiles whistled past his nose. "Yikes!" He ducked and flinched when the needles whizzed through the house. "Hit the ice!"

All five FVI members dropped low during the bombardment. Then they popped back up and looked around. Like Jacob, they could see the multiple layers of shadow trails the missiles created.

"What in all the snowballs is that?" a fairy asked.

"Who the hell are they?" Devyn asked.

"My helpers. Thanks the Frosti all of you came," Jacob said.

"We'll always answer the call of a Frost," one of the faeries said.

The five FVI members moved around the room.

"We'll manage the dark magic outside," one fairy said. The three fairies broke off and phased through the wall to put up a better defense against the missiles. They had the stronger white magic against the dark shadow attack.

"Greetings, sir, seems that you're having a bit of trouble," the highest-ranking elf said. "Aspen, Lord Jacob, at your service. This is my partner, Lixue."

The other elf offered a respectful bow. "Greetings, Lord Jacob."

"Thank you for your prompt response to my call. That is putting things a bit mild, but, yes, a touch of trouble. This is my crystal partner, Devyn. The needles are for him. The only mortal," Jacob said.

"My bad!" Devyn said with a smile and wave.

"Really?"

"What?" Devyn shrugged. "Good to meet both of you. I'm out of my element here. Big time! Not freaking out. I swear."

With a roll of his eyes, Jacob returned his attention to the elves. "The fairies can only hold them off for a few moments."

"They should have—"

"They're from the Yule Lads."

"Sweet frozen icicles, that's powerful black magic," Aspen said with a shudder. "Nasty creatures. Are they after your crystal partner?"

"That's the question we're trying to answer."

"Where is the CPD? There should have been an alarm with such a massive attack upon a Frost and a mortal," Aspen said.

"There seems to be an issue with the Boston office. I have a CPD friend looking into that because of a separate problem. Until they show up—" Another volley of ammunition ripped through during the pause. Jacob looked around his violated home. "We can't stay here."

"No shit."

"Not helping, Dev."

"Shit!" Devyn ducked lower at another salvo. "Damn... how can they create so many damn needle things?"

"Ooh, fairies missed a few," Aspen said while Lixue redirected them with a wave of his hand. "He's a half fairy."

"Can you—"

"Take care of things here. Aye. We'll clean up and forward anything you need. Going to your NPD home?"

"That's the plan. There will be stronger defensive measures there until we can figure out what in the name of Frosti is happening."

"Excellent plan. If someone from the CPD appears, we'll send them your way."

"Good. Thanks."

"Best hurry, sir," Aspen said. "Pleasure to meet you, Crystal Partner Devyn."

"Umm. Yeah. Same. Still learning about all this. Sorry," Devyn said.

"Lots to learn and even more to enjoy," Aspen said.

Keeping low, Jacob moved toward the chair, yanked his messenger bag off, and slung the strap over one shoulder. Then he returned to where Devyn continued to hide. "Heart. Watch. To me!" He held out his hand toward the living room. When the crystal heart, the golden pin, and pocket watch flew to his hand, he slipped them into an outer pocket on the bag. Then he wind-milled his arm around them with a spell upon his lips.

Standing upon his base of power, he pulled on his energy and strength. Though he held enough to not fully transform into his Frost persona, just his skin and hair remained altered. He built a thick protective wall of ice and snow and pushed as much bright winter magic into the barrier to prevent more shadowy bullets pouring through the kitchen to give them much needed time. It would support everything the FVI members did to assist them.

"Impressive, Lord Jacob," Lixue said.

"That should give you something to hold and use as a barrier." Jacob reached for the box and pulled it down. Then he flipped open the bag's flap and tucked the box inside the larger internal pocket. He closed and locked the flap. Kneeling on the floor by Devyn, he pulled out the heart and watch. Against his better judgment, he recognized the need for Devyn to keep them close for the journey. He held out the precious items toward Devyn.

"What are you doing?"

"Take hold of the heart and watch. Keep them close and don't—"

"Drop the heart. Yeah, I got that part figured out. Don't smash the crystal heart into itty bitty shards. Otherwise it would be really, really bad."

"Extremely bad for everyone. Especially me."

"Got it. Okay? I got it. Promise." Devyn took the objects and slid the watch into one pocket. He held the heart close to his belly. Then he winced at another salvo and ducked his head. "Jacob—"

"Lixue!" Aspen called out.

"Will cover the hole," Lixue said while he moved to throw up another volley of snow and ice. "Sir, I must insist that you leave. Now!"

"We're getting out of here. I promise. Hold on." Jacob slid his hand back into the messenger bag and pulled out a velvet bag. From inside, he selected a snow globe leftover from his preparations to pull Devyn out of Boston. He shook and activated it with his magic.

"Jacob—"

"Trust me. We'll be safe."

Devyn nodded.

Jacob stared at the globe. "North Pole Dimension. Frost Ridge. Serac home. Living room." He sent a pulse of his magic activate the globe. When blue light and snow swirled inside the glass, he tossed the globe to the side to shatter it.

A swirl of blue magic opened within their protective area and twisted into a portal.

"Take my hand and we're stepping through. Nothing will happen to you because you're Cheimon. I promise," Jacob said while he rose and held out his free hand. He kept his other hand wrapped around the bag's strap.

"What about the house? Our things?"

"Once we leave, the attackers will stop their barrage. Nothing else will be damaged. They can't physically or magically pass through my wards, but I can't risk the chance one of those volleys hitting you."

"I'll take some damage."

"Or worse. Please, Devyn, I will answer your questions and concerns when we get to safety. Right now, we need to move."

"Go on with him, Crystal Partner. We'll cover everything here and forward your belongings to the NPD," Aspen said.

"Please, come with me, Devyn."

Devyn stood and took Jacob's hand. He cuddled the heart close to his chest. "With you."

Nodding, Jacob moved them toward and through the portal.

Chapter Six

They reappeared in a tidy living room. The portal closed behind them with a poof of sparkles and snowflakes.

Devyn wobbled and pressed a hand to his belly. He burped low and meaty. "Whoa... That was something."

Jacob placed a hand against Devyn's back to support him. "Sorry about that. The first-time portaling can have that effect on travelers. I forgot to warn you."

"Add a full belly on top of it?"

"Nauseous?"

"Big time. Seas rolling bad. Yeah." With another belch, Devyn grimaced and glanced at Jacob. "Hey, you're back to normal. Good. Whoa... Another roll there."

"Mistletoe!" Jacob shouted.

"Season's greetings, Lord Jacob. Greetings, chosen crystal heart bearer," Mistletoe said in a cheerful tone when he entered the room. He wore white stockings with an evergreen needle pattern, deep green knee pants, a white shirt with flowy sleeves, a light green vest, and finished with soft brown ankle boots. He stood around five feet tall with dark curly hair and bright green eyes filled with a cheery mirth.

"Wow! Bright combination!" Devyn belched again and wiggled a few fingers. Then he passed the heart over to Jacob to place a hand against his mouth. Another meaty belch escaped. "Oh, dear God, that didn't taste good."

Jacob slid the bag's strap over his head and carefully placed it on one of the side tables. Then he opened the flap, pulled out the box that held his various NPD items, and set it down. He kept part of his attention on the heart Devyn held close to his belly.

"Oh, sweet snowflakes, not a good first-time traveler. I'll fetch some peppermint crackle. It'll fix you in a jiffy," Mistle said. He hurried off in a different direction.

"Who or what was that?" Devyn asked around another series of burps.

"Just concentrate on one spot and breathe slow. Calm yourself down. The peppermint will calm your stomach," Jacob said. "That is my house elf, Mistletoe Jangle. He takes care of my NPD place and other things when I'm away from the NPD. Sort of my assistant, but much more responsibility goes with his position."

"This is your—" A belch interrupted. "Your NPD home?"

"Yes, it is an open-floor design with bedrooms upstairs, a large office on one end, and a comfortable large kitchen. Also, I added an attached apartment for Mistle off the kitchen. When I built my home on the island, I kept the same design but made it a little smaller."

"Here it is. Fresh peppermint crackle. Chew on this and let it sit in your cheek for a few extra moments before you swallow. The extract will help soothe your belly. With the extra benefit that it tastes so yummy," Mistle said when he returned with a small plate. A pile of bright green and brown squares were in the middle of the golden bell decorated plate.

"'Preciate it," Devyn mumbled while he took a few pieces and crammed them in his mouth.

"Sit down too." Jacob cupped Devyn's elbow and helped him into a plush deep blue armchair.

Devyn loudly chewed and sucked on the crackle with a few milder belches.

Mistle set the plate on the table next to Devyn's chair. "In case you need more. If this doesn't work, a spot of peppermint and honey tea will finish the remedy. You'll be back to jiffy and perky in no time."

Closing his eyes, Devyn wiggled his fingers and leaned back in the chair. He rubbed his free hand against his lower stomach. "Rolling belly is so not a good feeling. Hate nausea."

"Sorry. I forgot about the possible side effect of an emergency portal travel. They're not as stable sometimes," Jacob said. "This is your first time through the dimensional shield. Luckily, you must have been registered. Otherwise—"

"Otherwise? What? What? Don't stop there."

"Umm. Don't worry about it. Nothing happened. No need to go through all the details since it didn't happen." Jacob crouched next to him. He brushed his fingers through Devyn's soft hair. "I'm truly sorry about all of this trouble."

"Not your fault... 'Dem bad guys did it. So bad," Devyn mumbled. He turned his head and kissed Jacob's inner arm when it brushed his face. The only part he could reach without moving and aggravating his current condition. Then he held out the heart. "Best for you to keep this."

"Are you sure?"

"Yup. Might be nap time. 'Gain."

"Okay," Jacob said when he took the heart, shrank it down with a bit of magic, and slid it into a pocket.

"Hate 'dem bad guys. So bad," Devyn mumbled with a yawn.

"Bad guys? Lord Jacob, what happened?" Mistle asked.

"One of the Yule Lads connected and focused upon Devyn at his workplace and continued to bother him these last three years. They gave him a 'present' which kept him within their contact. A crew of Yules' lackeys attacked my island home a few moments ago. I don't think one of them was there. The energy wasn't dark or strong enough for their presence. I need to speak with the Council. They have to know what is happening," Jacob said. "I left a team of FVI agents fighting back."

"Speaking of the Council, you have a scroll. It popped out of a portal from the CPD," Mistletoe said and pointed to the coffee table.

Jacob picked up the scroll. "I'm expecting a mirror call from the CPD."

"Of course, Lord Jacob."

Cracking the CPD seal, Jacob unrolled the scroll. Then he smiled while he read the contents.

Devyn cracked open his eyes. "What's 'dat?"

"Congratulations, Devyn, you're a registered Cheimon elf. They managed to narrow things down along the elf line. Looks like you come from the tinkerers. Kind of funny considering you're an engineer." Jacob turned the scroll to show him. "This is kind of like a Cheimon birth certificate and registration rolled into one."

Devyn glanced over the cheery looking form filled with golden lettering, holly leaves and berries, and flourishing signatures. "Keep it safe for me?"

"Of course." Jacob rolled it up and Mistletoe created a red ribbon for him to tie it together. "Thanks. Add this to the safe in my office."

"Will do," Mistle said. He snapped his fingers and the scroll disappeared into his private dimensional fold for storage.

A tingling of jingle bells rang through the room.

"That would be the mirror," Mistle said and snapped his fingers.

A silver-rimmed standing mirror appeared next to him.

"Whoa—" Devyn said.

"Mistletoe has some extra special powers while in the house," Jacob said.

"One of the many pleasures of my position." Mistle hit the buttons. "Jacob Serac's NPD home. This is Mistletoe, resident house elf, speaking."

The mirror's face changed to reflect Strike's face. The background was another CPD office.

"Mistletoe, greetings, this is Strike, CPD Agent — Alaska, but currently in Boston. Is Jacob there?" Strike asked.

"Right here, Strike," Jacob said and moved into view.

"What in the name of Blitzen's lightning is happening? A major alarm went off in your cabin's location. I shipped off an advance team there. They discovered a mess outside along with three fairies and two elves standing guard. You weren't there, nor was your crystal heart partner," Strike said.

"We had a visit from some goons from the Yule Lads. They shot through the walls and my barriers with these—" Jacob paused while he pulled out the protected needle from his pocket and removed the frost. With his magic, he floated it above his palm and spun it to show it off to Strike. "They were sent with a shadow magic to infiltrate anything and search only for mortal flesh."

"Only one mortal in the cabin," Devyn called out. "My bad!"

"Since he's up and speaking, I take it nothing hit him," Strike asked.

"We're okay. I called on some FVI help when I realized what was happening. The fairies blocked most of the shadow magic, while the elves helped us make our escape. I captured one of these for analysis."

"That's helpful. How in the name of Blitzen's lightning did they find you? Let alone land on your island. No one knows where it is. Right?"

"That's what I thought. It's hidden within a specialized NPD and Frost dimension pocket."

"Umm... My bad? I think..." Devyn managed to push himself out of the chair, but he fell to his knees. "Oops. Still dizzy. Okay. Need to keep moving." Then he crawled over to the mirror.

"Are you okay? I thought you were feeling better when I left," Strike asked.

"Portal sickness. Not been a good day for my mortal." Jacob helped Devyn adjust himself into a sitting position.

"Oh, cookie crumbles." Mistletoe snatched and placed pillows behind Devyn's butt and back. "You should at least be comfortable if you insist on sitting on the floor."

"Thanks, Mistle." Devyn pulled the watch from his pocket. "I think there might be more than a spell on this watch."

"Like what?" Strike asked.

"A tracker, of some sort, hidden within the mechanism. It could allow them to track me, no matter where I went, especially if they used your version of technology to get through the dimensions."

"Interesting thought," Strike said. "Good suggestion. Wouldn't put it past the Yule Lads to add something extra to a 'gift.' At least, something beyond that blasted spell of theirs."

"Anything about the spell?"

"Early diagnostic from the R&D team, it's a nasty piece of work. Skillfully woven and designed to work over an extended period time to remain undetectable."

"Wonderful news," Jacob grumbled. "How would we figure out what else is attached to the watch?"

"Could you help me find someone with some tools? I could take it apart and figure it out with another NPD engineer? I am part tinkerer, you said, perhaps I could go to their office," Devyn said.

"No, you need to rest—"

"Jacob, we need to figure out what happened. I caused these problems when I accepted the watch as a gift. Let me help. This, at least, I know what I'm doing," Devyn interrupted. "I'll be okay. Give me a cup of that peppermint tea Mistletoe recommended, a bit of food, and a pair of boots. I can't go out in my slippers."

"I can take care of that part," Mistletoe said.

"Excellent. Thanks, Mistletoe," Devyn said. "We're safe in the NPD from any further attacks. Right?"

"According to the rules, the Yule Lads can enter the NPD, because they belong there," Strike said. "Though, they can't enter NP Center without an invitation or someone creating a hole in the protective barrier and wards."

"What's the Center?" Devyn asked.

"The beating heart and center of the NPD. There are multiple villages around the main beacon and pole. You can see it when we leave my home," Jacob said. He looked to Strike. "What do you think?"

"That it's a great idea. The Yules would think of something crazy like a tracker. Let him figure it out. We can concentrate on the other problems," Strike said. "Once I finish here, I'll head to the Center. If the Yules are planning something major with the Winter Solstice Event, I'll alert the rest of the CPD agents to get there for added protection. We should also contact the Nutcrackers and Toy Soldiers to place them on high alert. Even bring in the Mouse King and his crew. We should stand together for a meeting at the CPD Headquarters and lay out what we know."

"Agreed, though I'm not sure how much they'll understand or accept. I better also check out the Ice Cavern and see what happened to the other Frosts. If there are shadows in their hearts, then this isn't the first time the Yule Lads struck and they're definitely planning something."

"Are the hearts kept?"

"This isn't information to be repeated. Are you alone?" Jacob asked.

"Understood. I'm the only one in the mirror room."

"Good. Each shattered heart is kept because they hold memories and magic. A Frost will create a new crystal upon wakening to connect it to a new partner," Jacob said. "Frosts maintain vigilance and protection over the Cavern because those hearts are precious and hold immense power."

"That's interesting to know. Something I'm sure the Lads will want to figure out a way to take the power for themselves."

"Unless invited or connected to a Frost, no one else can enter or even locate the Cavern. An additional protective measure. The Cavern will be my next stop after the meeting and dropping off the needle. If I see shadows, I'll alert—"

"Retrieval specialists from CPD. They'll arrive with globes and remove the spells from each heart. They'll send all the globes to R&D for investigation and disposal. I don't want to leave a single shadow spell lingering anywhere within the Center."

"Same here. Without the spells, perhaps most of the Frosts will reawaken quicker because it wasn't a natural shattering. Not sure. That might depend on contacting the Spirit of Winter."

"Why would anyone want to attack the Frosts?" Devyn asked.

"I'm not sure. Each Cheimon division and bloodline are connected to the NPD. The top three are the Frosts, the Clauses, and the fairies. They connect to the three NPD ancients who created everything. Our lines flow from them and share power and magic. If one line weakens..." Jacob trailed off and looked at Strike.

"The Yules could enter during Winter Solstice Event and destroy the beacon," Strike finished.

"What's the Winter Solstice Event?" Devyn asked.

"It's a marvelous, magical even," Mistletoe said in a wondrous tone. He smiled and clapped his hands. "The Event happens when the magical beacon, the beating heart of the NPD, becomes renewed with energy and magic by the Solstice Sun. It's a magnificent ball where everyone dresses in their finest and attends. Our magic comes from the beacon. Without the renewal, the beacon is in danger of weakening, dropping the barrier, and revealing us to the mortal world."

"When does this take place?"

"Sunday night. This Sunday night. It's even more popular than Christmas around here. Winter Solstice belongs to the NPD. Christmas is for the mortals, but their belief and love of the holiday helps to strengthen our realm," Mistletoe said.

"Oh, sweet frosty icicles," Jacob said.

"Blitzen's lightning. They're after the freaking beacon!" Strike dragged a hand through his hair. "Everyone is going to get an alert. Get your ass and that needle to the CPD. We'll need an antidote if they use it. I'll meet you there for the meeting if I can get this office under control. Then get to the Cavern."

"Will do," Jacob said.

"Devyn, do whatever you can to figure out that watch."

"Got it," Devyn said.

"We're going to need a lot of power to stop this. And a plan. I'll contact Kringle for a meeting. But we need... evidence, proof..."

"I'll work on that. Promise. Just get here," Jacob said.

"Will do. Excellent work, you two." With that, Strike ended the call.

The mirror darkened.

The three of them stared at their reflections.

"Oh, sweet Christmas pudding, this is bad," Mistletoe said. "Even worse than the Great Ash Poof Event."

"What? He capitalized that, didn't he?" Devyn asked.

"He did," Jacob said with a sigh.

"Why? What happened?"

"Mistle..."

"What? It's far far worse. Sweet pudding and cookie crumbles." Mistletoe worried his hands together.

"Oh, come on, now you really have to tell me what happened," Devyn said. He wiggled on the pillows to get comfortable, snatched the mug to sip at the tea, and munched on the ginger crumbles.

"There's no time—"

"Please?"

"Okay. Go ahead, Mistle..."

"What?" the house elf squeaked.

"You brought it up. You tell it," Jacob said and crossed his arms.

"Oh, cookie crumbles," the elf muttered.

"Running out of precious time."

"Yes. Yes. Can't rush the telling of a tale."

"Mistle—"

Mistletoe waved a hand at him.

Devyn pushed himself off he cushions and moved back to the chair. He popped a few more crumbles in his mouth.

The elf perched at the end of another chair. "This happened when I first came to work and live within Lord Jacob's home. Many many years ago."

"Mistle—"

The elf waved him off. "This is the first time I lived within a Frost's home. They are quite different from a regular NPD home, but I didn't understand how unique, because I grew up and trained in elf homes."

"Unique?" Devyn asked.

"Frosts use magic to build their homes in the NPD. I built the walls with snow, ice, and live trees. The snow hardens to cement and holds form. The trees bend and form to the magic to add to the support. Because of my magic and the energy of NPD, the house retains an... inherent..." Jacob paused.

"Alive. The house is sentient," Mistletoe finished.

"Sentient?" Devyn asked.

Mistletoe nodded. "Because of this, there are certain quirks throughout the house that I needed to know. One of them is there will be branches sprouting out from limbs and wooden mantles. I was trying to organize and tidy up Lord Jacob's office. There is a small fireplace to keep him warm on the extra chilly winter evenings. Even for a Frost, I like to keep a light fire going to keep a toasty atmosphere. I found a branch grew on the corner of the mantle. Thinking nothing about it, I clipped off the branch and went on with my cleaning.

"Rumblings and odd noises echoed throughout the room and house. I didn't understand what was happening. I could tell something was happening inside the fireplace and flue. Perhaps a bird or a critter crawled up inside and would pop out at me. Alas, no, it was far worse. All of the sudden—POOF!" Mistletoe made a movement with his hands.

"POOF?"

Mistletoe didn't respond.

"The fireplace spewed a massive amount of ash and soot into the room in a humongous cloud that covered everything," Jacob said.

Devyn's jaw dropped.

Mistletoe dropped his head into his hands.

"I walked in moments after when I heard the rumblings. The entire office from ceiling to floor was black. I mean deep soot black. I could only find Mistletoe when he opened his eyes and coughed. Then I noticed the branch clipping in his hand. I asked if he cut the branch, he said yes, and I told him don't do it again. I explained about the house."

"So. So. So bad. Horrible. Worse resident house elf ever," Mistletoe said.

Devyn dropped back in the chair. Laughing.

They waited him out.

When he caught his breath, he managed to ask, "How..." Then he slipped into another round of laughter. Getting back under a bit of control, he held up his hands to finish his question. "How did you clean up?"

"Oh, first I had to apologize to the house. Then, I clicked my fingers with a bit of energy and all the ash and soot was gone. Spotless. I even used a bit of my mother's fairy magic to reattach the branch and nurtured the break. Since then, I ask the house what it needs and listen to everything," Mistletoe said. "Lesson very well learned and never to be forgotten."

Devyn laughed again.

"All right. All right. There is work to be done," Jacob said and clapped his hands to get things under control.

Devyn cleared his throat, laughed, and tried again. "Of course. Yes. I umm... need something else to..." He moved his slippers around. "Not quite dressed to make an appearance."

"Right. Mistletoe, could you help him into some appropriate clothes? Nothing to flashy, please," Jacob said.

"Of course! Oh no! Cookie crumbles and dirty flakes!" Mistletoe gasped when he stared at Devyn.

"What? What is it?" Devyn asked. "What?"

Jacob sighed. "What is it now, Mistle?"

"What is he going to wear to the Winter Solstice Event? He can't go like that! I would be the laughingstock of all the house elves. No, no, no, this is far more than simple slippers. I must fix all of this," Mistle said while he waved at Devyn's comfortable outfit and slippers.

"Umm— Jacob?" Devyn said.

"Oh, good melting icicles," Jacob muttered.

Chapter Seven

When Mistletoe finally deemed them presentable to step outside the home and with promises of a set of — in Mistletoe's words — fantabulous sparkling matching outfits for the Event, Jacob managed to remind Mistletoe about the FVI agents that would pop in with their belongings from the cabin. Then he hustled Devyn out of the home before Mistletoe could delay them again.

"So, Mistletoe is a trip. I like him. A lot. Keeps you on your toes," Devyn teased.

"Don't start. House elves, sheesh," Jacob said. "Just don't get on their bad side, because it isn't what you expect."

"Mistletoe has a bad side?"

Jacob shuddered.

Devyn chuckled. "Oh... Where is the heart?"

"I have it. You gave it to me when you were a little out of it." Jacob pulled out a shrunken version of his crystal heart from a pocket.

"Can I have it back?"

"I need to show it to the NPD and the Cavern. When it is the right time, I will offer it back to you, but—" Jacob trailed off, not sure where to go next.

"It needs to heal. Along with us," Devyn said.

"That's right. I hope you enjoy learning more about my home and the Dimension." Jacob pocketed the heart back inside one of the jacket's multiple inner pockets hidden within the lining. He placed the frost-covered needle in one of the pockets. Instead of the messenger bag, he transferred a few items to the hip-length brown leather jacket he preferred to wear when in the Center.

Looking down the street, Jacob whistled to alert one of the sleigh taxis. "Here's our ride. Best way to travel through the Center."

A reindeer-driven sleigh jangled to a stop. A cheery elf tipped his hat. "Welcome home to the NPD, Lord Jacob. Greetings and good morning to your fellow. We're having a fine morning in the Center."

"Morning? What? How is that? We were eating a late lunch back at the cabin," Devyn said.

"Time moves different up here. We actually have two days to the Winter Solstice, not one," Jacob said. He waved hello to the driver.

"That's crazy. How do you keep track?" Devyn asked.

"Practice and I have a watch that tracks mortal and Dimension times. I'm often dashing in an out of the Dimensions when things pick up for my position. I oversee all the winter weather events from Greenland to the Carolinas and inland to the Great Lakes and Mississippi River. Because of my strength and age, I have one of the largest regions. The FVI members help, but I must oversee and divert them to specific areas when needed due to weather patterns." Jacob helped Devyn into the sleigh and climbed in next to him. Then he covered their laps with the cozy warmed blanket.

"Where can I take you fellows this fine morning?" their driver asked.

"Tinkerer HQ," Jacob said.

"On our way." The driver jingled the reins and clicked to get the reindeer pair trotting along the light snow-covered ground.

"Those aren't—" Devyn asked.

"Shifting reindeer? No. Only regular ones," Jacob said.

"Just checking. Didn't want to make a mistake." Devyn leaned forward and looked around their surroundings. "This is beautiful. Where are we?"

"We're leaving Frost Ridge, where all the Frosts make their homes. Some are single homes and others are either villas, townhomes, or apartments. All depends on what they desire. The lower-level Frosts work together to create the multi-family buildings."

"Are all of them sentient?"

"No, only the higher-level Frost homes are sentient. That's mostly due to our age and how long we have been Frosts," Jacob said.

The sleigh continued along the path down the hill that overlooked the rest of NPD Center.

"Look at all the colors. This is brilliant and amazing, almost like all those movies about Santa and his workshop village," Devyn said about the gingerbread brown homes with candy cane stripes, holly green, cranberry red, and all other holiday colors and styles as decorations. "Who lives here?"

"This is Candy Land Corner, the village for most of the elves who work throughout the Center."

"Not Mistletoe."

"No, he's a resident house elf, which means he lives on the premises of the home he cares. According to the house elves, it's a higher and more prestigious position, especially if they work for a Frost, Kringle, or one of the higher reindeer families. Other house elves come and go throughout the week. Because I don't live here permanently, I rather someone stay at the house to protect it and keep up the energy."

"It doesn't like to be lonely."

"Nope. Terrible things happen if no one is there. I found that out the difficult way before deciding to hire Mistletoe." Jacob shook his head. "Melted walls. Flooding. Branches overgrown everywhere. All kinds of trouble, unexpected maintenance, and expensive care."

"Your home throws temper tantrums."

"If left alone for any length of time, yes," Jacob said. "It's rather surprising how well you're taking all of this in and accepting it. Are you accepting it?"

Devyn waved a hand to point out the colorful village. "This... All of this. It's... breathtaking. Insane. Almost unbelievable. But—" He shook his head. "I believe it. I believe you. I don't understand about everything you do with your gifts, but—" He touched Jacob's cheek. "I believe."

Jacob captured Devyn's hand and kissed his fingers. "Thank you. I needed to hear that." With those words and acceptance, Jacob felt a minor crack heal within the heart and their connection. Things were being repaired between them.

"I'm sorry I couldn't tell you sooner. With or without the spell, I apologize for pulling away. I didn't realize it was happening." Devyn closed his fingers around Jacob's hand to hold tight. "It was never my intention or desire to pull away from you, even when it was happening. You know how much I love you."

"I love you too, Devyn. We'll figure out the next steps together. The first one is telling you the truth about me, about the crystal, and where I'm from."

"Promise?"

"Promise," Jacob said and added another kiss to Devyn's fingers. "Oh, look, here is Market Village. Everything and anything you need can be found here in these shops. This is the Main Street, but the market expands for two more streets on either side. There's also villas, apartments, and townhomes spread throughout for those who don't want to live in another village area."

"This is all so crazy, but beautiful," Devyn said. "I wish we had time to explore. After we save the world, right?"

"Right. Gotta save the world first. Even if they don't know about it."

"Typical oblivious world." Devyn chuckled.

Laughing with him, Jacob tucked Devyn under one arm while he pointed out different shops, taverns, and boutiques he frequented when in the NPD.

"That's where I had your pin designed for the heart," Jacob said and pointed to the jewelers. "It's also where I picked up that pen set you use at work."

"Really? Will the pin be fixed? I noticed that you picked it up from the table before we left."

"I can slip the heart back into the setting. It's connected to my magic," Jacob said to assure him. "I left the setting back at the house in my messenger bag. Mistletoe will keep it safe."

"Good to know."

Within a few moments, the driver pulled the sleigh to a stop in front of one of a series of large snow-built buildings with gingerbread roofs. "Tinkerer HQ, Lord Jacob."

"Thank you so much. A truly pleasant ride," Jacob said while he climbed down and helped Devyn out. He pulled out a few NPD ice-based coins from his pocket and handed over the correct amount.

"Will that be all for you today?"

"I need to go to Cheimon HQ, but I can walk there," Jacob said.

"Greetings and have a pleasant day," the driver said and clicked to the reindeer to get moving.

"Those are not regular coins," Devyn said. He slipped his hand into Jacob's pocket and looked at them. "Are these made out of ice?"

"What else would you expect of the Dimension coins?"

"Don't they melt."

"No, this is forever ice, a special magical property and mixed with flecks of copper, silver, or gold to designate the coins. The copper ones are dominion pennies. The silver coins are called lunar silver. The gold coins are chrono riyal. One hundred dominion pennies equal one lunar silver. Ten lunar silver equal one chrono riyal. If you don't have coins, the shops and drivers work on credit. If Mistle or I aren't with you, tell someone to charge it to my account." Jacob portioned out a few coins and handed them to Devyn. "Keep these with you." Then he created a card that had his name and address on it. "Also, take this card. Anyone questions you, hand them this card and they'll respond to my magic or contact me."

"Got it. Expecting trouble?"

"Just in case or unexpected events," Jacob said. "It's difficult to reach me when I'm at the Cavern, so the card will connect to Mistle if I'm out of range."

"Understood." Devyn tucked the card and coins into an inner pocket of the deep green jacket Mistletoe gave him. He looked around them and up at the colorful building looming over them. "Wow."

"Welcome to the infamous Toy Workshop of Santa Claus," Jacob said. "Only this is the reality, not a fairytale."

Devyn looked around, studied the multitude of elves, fairies, and other beings heading in and out of the different buildings. "Not quite what I expected."

"The workshop is divided into multiple buildings, each dedicated to a specific position or division. Collectively, they work together as a whole to create almost anything you can imagine. They quietly influence the mortal world for the new products." Jacob led the way up the steps and opened one door for Devyn.

"Is that how it works?"

"One of the many ways NPD influences and protects the mortal world. Since the creation of this place eons ago." Jacob checked a directory board and moved down the hallway to one of the main offices and laboratories nestled within the multi-storied building. Reaching the door, he entered the reception and smiled at the cheerful female elf behind the desk. "Greetings."

"Greetings. How may I help you today?" she asked.

"My name is Jacob Serac, American NE Frost. I'm hoping I could introduce my crystal partner, Devyn Risher, to the Head Tinkerer. There is a little project Devyn requires a bit of help from an elf expert to figure out," Jacob said.

"Oh, sweet cookies, I never met a Frost before. Greetings, my name is Starlight. Please allow me to contact my boss, Rusty Magicmoon," Starlight said and clicked a button on her headset.

"Does that always happen to you?" Devyn whispered to Jacob.

"Unfortunately."

"Big stuff on campus. Huh?"

"Please. Just another Cheimon scion."

"Not the way everyone acts around you," Devyn said and whistled under his breath. He rocked back on his heels with a playful grin.

Jacob knocked their shoulders together.

"Mister Rusty, a Lord Jacob Serac, a Frost scion, is here with his crystal partner, to speak with you. Yes, sir. Cookies, sir, I know. Isn't it thrilling?" Her voice rose high with the last question.

Devyn whistled again.

Jacob glared at him to make him stop.

"Yes, sir. Will send them through." She clicked off and smiled at them. Then she rose to step toward the double office doors with a gold and green sign announcing the 'Head Tinkerer.' "Would you like something to eat and drink? I have some yummy warm apple cider and fresh cookies."

"Those would be wonderful. I'm not going to stay, though," Jacob said and looked at Devyn.

"Of course. I'm always up to try some delicious treats. I'll happily accept the offer of cider and cookies. Thank you," Devyn said.

"Glutton," Jacob muttered.

"Proud of it." Devyn rubbed his belly. "It's been a rough day."

With a bird twitter of a laugh, Starlight opened the door. "Excellent. I shall bring a tray in for everyone to share." She leaned inside and called out. "Mister Rusty! Lord Jacob Serac and his crystal partner, Devyn, are entering."

"Welcome! Welcome! Come on back," a jolly deep voice called out from somewhere deep within the room.

Jacob led Devyn into the expanded office and laboratory filled with tables, cabinets, and a long wall of windows to let the sunshine pour through to highlight all the gizmos, gadgets, gears, tools, supplies, and projects in progress spread throughout the room.

"Wow," Devyn said under his breath. "Engineer wonderland."

With a soft chuckle, Jacob guided Devyn through the vast room. "Don't get distracted by all the potential sparklies. You can investigate all you want at another time. First, you need to figure out the watch."

"Watch right. Ooh, look at that—" Devyn said, but stopped when Jacob tugged him along. "What— Oh, sorry, can't help it. Watch. Right." He cleared his throat to redirect his attention.

An elf met them halfway. Dressed in dark boots, trousers with candy-cane stripe suspenders, a deep green button-down shirt, with a long brown vest overlay, the elf was the epitome of the NPD elves. Not too short. Not too tall. Not a crazy amount of hair. Though, his green eyes were bright and cheery behind the gold-rimmed glasses perched on his nose.

"Greetings, Lord Jacob and Devyn, a pleasure to welcome you to my humble tinkerer's laboratory. I'm Rusty Magicmoon, Head Tinkerer," the elf said and held out a hand.

Jacob shook hands. "Pleasure to meet you, Mister Rusty."

"Rusty, please," he said.

"I'm Jacob. This is my crystal partner, Devyn."

Rusty shook hands with Devyn. "Never met a crystal partner before."

"Devyn comes with a few extras in his bloodline, like a line of tinkerers. It's why he was able to travel to NPD with me today," Jacob said.

"Please excuse anything wrong with my manners or what I might say or do, Rusty. I'm learning about everything, starting today," Devyn said. "You're not what I expected—"

"You mean one of those tiny creatures darting around in the stories?"

"Well, yes," Devyn said.

Rusty laughed. "Not for many centuries. We all changed over time to accommodate the modern times."

Devyn flushed.

"No worries, young one, ask all your questions—"

"First, we should explain why we're here. Though, this must be kept in confidence until the top three are told what is happening," Jacob said.

"Of course, Jacob, come further inside and be seated. My walls are sound and magic proof. Nothing can get in or out," Rusty said and led them to a sitting area.

Jacob settled with Devyn. Then he leaned forward and explained everything that happened to them up to that point. He paused his story when he heard Starlight entering to deliver the tray of cider and cookies. When she left, he finished the story that brought them to Rusty's office.

"Sweet turning gears, that's a wild story. One I wouldn't put past those dastardly Yule Lads. May I inspect this watch?" Rusty asked.

"Of course." Devyn pulled out the watch and handed it to Rusty. "I believe there is a tracking device of some type, perhaps magical, hidden within the gears. I require help and tools to open the watch and pull out the device."

"What happens if we find one?" Rusty asked.

"It would need to be given to the Research team at the CPD marked for Agent Strike's attention. R&D will also get involved if needed," Jacob said.

"Oh, of course, of course. Hmm. Lemme see..." Rusty popped in an eye loupe while he examined the watch. "Exquisite artisanship. Excellent metalwork. Design. Lovely gears. Yes. Yes. Lovely watch."

"Here is how to check out the inside." Devyn leaned closer and popped the catch to open the watch.

"May I leave Devyn in your care, Rusty? I have other matters to attend too," Jacob said.

Rusty pulled his attention from the watch. "Yes. Yes. He can stay with me."

"Due to the instability of the issue with the Lads."

"We are quite secure here. Extra warding and protective measures."

"No one will be allowed to collect him other than myself."

"Jacob, just send Mistletoe—" Devyn said.

"No, Devyn, I'm not taking any chances with your life. Even here in the heart of the NPD," Jacob said.

"Could I suggest using a code word or phrase to prove someone will come from you? I would use that as a protective measure to release him in their care if you're unable to return or alert the authorities there is a breach," Rusty offered.

"That would be appreciated." Jacob thought a moment and leaned over to whisper an ancient Frost phrase in Rusty's ear. "Got it?"

Rusty nodded. He tapped a finger to his temple. "Locked in. I shall keep Devyn in my care. Lots to show a new tinkerer. Once we figure out this interesting puzzle of a problem."

"Wonderful." Jacob leaned over to place a kiss on Devyn's temple. "Keep safe. Please."

"I will. Even if I have a bit of fun," Devyn said.

"I'm sure you'll find lots here to keep you well occupied. I'm not sure how long I will be, but please stay here unless I or Mistletoe fetch you."

"Of course. I understand the danger. Now, let us get to work."

With a nod, Jacob kissed Devyn's temple again. Then he rose and headed toward the door.

"Jacob…"

Turning when Devyn called his name, Jacob got an armful of Devyn. A little shocked, he wrapped his arms around his crystal partner. Then he felt another one of the cracks sealed within his crystal heart at the tender gesture. He rested his cheek upon Devyn's soft curls. "Miss having you in my arms," he whispered.

"Same here." Devyn pulled back a little. He placed his hand upon Jacob's cheek. "I know you're a big-bad-magical-Frost and all that shit, but please take care with my Jacob. He's a tender-hearted soul. One I would miss a lot if anything happened. That heart is a wee bit cracked."

Jacob smiled at the tenderness in Devyn's words. "I'll make sure to take care. Promise. No fighting the big baddies. Not without back-up."

With a nod, Devyn pressed a light kiss to Jacob's lips.

Jacob tightened his grip upon Devyn a bit more and let the kiss linger to a few more minutes. He missed the touch and taste of Devyn. With a final nuzzle, he pulled back.

A bit dazed from the attention, Devyn sighed and lifted to meet Jacob's gaze. "Ahh, definitely missed that. Please take care."

"I will. Promise."

"Good."

"Get back to your gears and devices that I know you're itching to touch and manipulate," Jacob teased.

With a laugh, Devyn released Jacob and returned to his spot by Rusty.

Rusty smiled over Devyn's head at Jacob. His eyes bright with emotion from the tender moment.

Heartened and stronger from the embrace, Jacob willed himself to leave the laboratory.

"Greetings again, Lord Jacob. Hope you enjoyed your visit. Where is your dear friend?" Starlight asked when he closed the door.

Jacob nodded to the assistant with a smile. "Thank you, I did enjoy it. Devyn will stay with Rusty for a while."

"Of course. I'll keep them supplied with warm drinks and lots of cookies," Starlight said.

Jacob pressed his fingers against the bridge of his nose. "There is more to this issue than cookies. Please follow the strictest protocol for any visitors."

"Visitors come and go all the time to speak with Master Rusty."

"I understand, but no one can enter the laboratory area while they are together. There is trouble surrounding the NPD. I need him protected."

"I understand, Mister Jacob. No visitors inside unless authorized by Master Rusty. Yes, sir, I'll make sure to remember those orders."

Jacob sincerely doubted the light-hearted elf understood how dangerous the situation could turn into if the Lads invaded the NPD. "Thank you."

Starlight waved. "Have a wonderful day."

Sliding his hands into the outer pockets, Jacob left the Tinkerer building and turned toward the CPD Headquarters located on the opposite side of the square. He let out a long breath.

Then a portal opened next to him.

Jacob jumped to one side. He called a massive snowball in one hand and ice in the other to fire upon his attacker.

Strike stepped out onto the street. "Ahh, the personal locator globe option worked. Wasn't connecting before so thought it might be faulty. Which is unusual with the R&D elves. Excellent," he said. "Hello, Jacob." He held up one hand. "Whoa— Don't fire that at me. I'm a good reindeer. Honest."

Grumbling at pesky reindeer and CPD agents, Jacob recalled the snow and ice. He shook his hands to remove the last droplets. "Don't sneak up on a Frost. Personal locator... What?"

"Personal locator globe. Something new I asked the R&D elves to create when I realized how I might have to locate you right away and get to your side. They used your genetic code to implant the eternal snowflakes. Then I would add those flakes to the globe and say your name. Crack the globe, open the portal, and here I am." Strike looked around. "Only, the portal didn't open right away."

"I was in the Tinkerer Head Office. It was protected."

"Ahh, that would do it. I'll let the elves know about that glitch. Perhaps they could add a specific kind of response that there is a protective shield or something," Strike said. "Is Devyn safe with Rusty?"

"He is. He's in his happy space with all those gears and tools. They're already diving into the watch and figure out if there's a locator beacon."

"Excellent. Rusty would have been the elf I told you to search out." Strike settled himself and adjusted his backpack and long coat. Then he studied Jacob. "You're looking a little stronger. Things going well?"

"Yes. Cracks are starting to heal. It was an excellent idea to explain everything to Devyn. Hiding all my secrets created more walls and barriers then I thought. It'll take time to fully heal the rift, but—" Jacob shrugged. "There is the hope and possibility that we saved our relationship in time. The spell caused things to disintegrate faster which alerted me."

"Hopefully, it gave us enough time to heal the rest of the Frosts and stop this invasion," Strike said. "I'm happy for the both of you."

"Thank you. Did you sort out the mess at Boston?"

"There's no sorting that out in this brief time. Lots of issues in that office, but Asher is on top of the situation. I have other reindeer and elves going through that place. I organized the primary functions to make them work and left the rest to the clean-up crew," Strike said.

"So much of that happening everywhere," Jacob said with a look over his shoulder at the building he left and the ambivalent female elf.

"I thought things were good." Strike lifted an eyebrow. "What's wrong with you to change that?"

"Oh, it has nothing to do with Devyn."

"Then what's wrong?"

"Something I notice every time I visit the NPD."

"Which is?"

"Why are some residents so cheerfully clueless about the outer world?"

"Because that is how they wish to live their lives in this cheery, no danger, no trouble, and wonderful domain. Especially the ones that don't have to leave the Dimension for the mortal realm. Not that all residents have things easy. There are still ethical, moral, and financial issues, but they ignore the dark parts. It's the nature of elves and fairies. Not everyone deals with the nasty side of things all the time, day in and out, all year around," Strike said.

"Even as a Frost, I can't get away from the dark corners."

"No one who works outside the Dimension can truly get away."

"And if the Lads break through the barriers on Winter Solstice?"

"All hell's lightning will break loose and burst this cheery bubble. Guess we better get working to save the Dimension," Strike said.

"Never ends. How long has it been since the last time someone dared to cross the barrier?"

"At least a century, but not from the Lads. Another of the ghastly ones from the shadows," Strike said. "The Lads are slipping."

"Or they were carefully planning this move."

"True. Their mama is a planner. Not one to cross."

"And Grýla loves her baby boys. Dark snow dump on that sorceress."

Laughing, Strike led the way to the other side of the square. They stopped to study a large building under construction off the one side of the CPD collection of buildings.

"What in the name of Blitzen's lightning is that?" Strike asked.

"Looks like a Frost building, but there are none in this area. We're all on the Ridge," Jacob said.

"Strange things happening in the NPD."

"Like always."

When they reached the HQ, Strike flashed his badge at the guardian trolls to gain them access. He led them straight to the Cheimon central hub where everything around the world and all dimensions was controlled.

"Let's see who responded to my distress call," Strike said when they reached the doors.

"And if they'll believe our insane story," Jacob said.

Chapter Eight

Entering the large room, it surprised them when they saw how full the room was packed with reindeer, elves, fairies, ælfs, and other members of the higher echelon of the CPD.

"This is what happens when you hit the all-call alert button," Krieg said when he appeared from the crowd, holding a pair of tablets in his arms. "Greetings, Mister Jacob, good to meet you in person."

"Blitzen's lightning! Didn't expect this response so fast," Strike said.

"The great Strike of Alaska called, so everyone hoofed it here. So many portals were happening at the same time. Insane. I'm surprised none of them crossed streams. That would be so bad," Krieg said.

"Hope you know what you're going to tell them," Jacob said.

"Me too," Krieg said.

Strike rolled his eyes. "Did you do the research I asked?"

"Yes. You're not going to like it."

"How bad?"

"Baaad," Krieg said.

"How bad?" Strike repeated.

"Systemic. All divisions have issues."

"Time to kick some tails, asses, and get their shit together before the whole thing falls apart. This is one of the reasons why I never visit here." Strike placed his hands together, linked his fingers, and pulled against them to crack his knuckles. Then he pointed to his brother. "Find the main computers and plug in. Get things ready—"

"May I inquire as to why one of my senior reindeer hit an all-call alert without informing me first?" a gentleman with a deep voice interrupted.

Swallowing hard when the booming voice cleared over all the rabble, Strike held still for a moment. "Lord Kringle, sir, greetings," he said.

"Icicles," Jacob muttered.

All three turned to face the latest Lord Kringle, the eldest Claus scion of Ded Moroz, to help rule over the dimension with the Lord of Winter, Jokul Frosti, and Mother Nature, Lady Gaia.

Standing over six-feet, Lord Kristophe Kringle VI was a well-built man with broad muscular shoulders, a strong chest, and long legs. Unlike the tales and songs, he didn't sport a rounded belly. For a day's work, he chose a forest-green button-down shirt with the sleeves rolled up his forearms, a velvet brown vest and trousers, and polished knee-high black boots. They stood so close that Strike could see the holly leaf embroidery in the velvet vest. The beloved deep red and white outfit only appeared during the Christmas celebrations. He kept his snow-white mustache and beard trimmed short. His white hair was long enough to curl around his shoulders with a few sweeping locks around the front. His bright blue eyes were usually full of cheer and laughter, but now they narrowed and darkened while he studied Strike.

"Lord Kringle, greetings, I didn't expect you to be here. I wanted to go over our findings and issues with the rest of the team before we spoke with the council," Strike said.

"We?"

Jacob stepped forward. "Me, sir."

"Jacob Serac, the America NE Frost and Jokul's top Frost. I heard you were back in the Dimension," Kringle said without asking Jacob anything. He lifted one dark eyebrow. "What are you doing mixed up with the CPD?"

A little surprised Lord Kringle would know him from all the other Frosts, Jacob found himself standing a little straighter under the powerful man's steady gaze. "I had an issue earlier with my crystal heart partner and Strike assisted me in correcting some problems. In turn, we discovered there is a deeper thread of danger running through what we initially thought was a simple problem about an estranged crystal partner."

"If you would let us speak with the CPD team, we will explain everything. Then you and the council can decide if the situation warrants further action," Strike said.

"This is breaking protocol—"

"Protocol wasn't created with this problem in mind, sir."

"What problem are we talking about?"

"A possible attack upon the Beacon by the Yule Lads on Winter Solstice," Strike said.

Kringle studied them, but his expression didn't reveal anything about his thoughts or reactions. "The Yule Lads? Do you have proof?"

"He's standing next to me and his crystal partner is here in the NPD," Strike said.

"Though, I believe that I'm not the first case," Jacob said.

"Your crystal partner is here?" Kringle asked. "How is that possible?"

"He has Cheimon blood. Forty-two percent," Jacob said. "Due to a strange reaction to a R&D concoction, Strike sampled my partner's blood. He's actually from a line of tinkerers and Dark Ælf."

"Definitely an unusual situation."

"If possible, I would like the historian elves to research if there were any other Cheimon-blooded crystal partners. If such a thing could have been recorded. Though, that's a request for a different time," Jacob said.

"Those elves record anything and everything. I will place a request to them to contact you with their results. I'm sure that will take some time and they will need to confer with the Spirit of Winter." Kringle tilted his head and closed his eyes. He nodded a couple of times. "Jokul will be here to speak with you personally, Jacob."

"I expected he would, sir," Jacob said.

"Sir—" Strike said. "May I address the group?"

"Go ahead." Kringle moved away to stand near the wall.

"Don't want to get on his bad side," Jacob muttered.

"Tell me about it," Strike said.

"Good luck."

Clearing his throat, Strike stepped toward the main center consoles where Krieg waited. "Greetings and thank you to all CPD agents and staff who responded to my alert. The situation we're facing has the potential to be grave and fraught with danger for our beloved Dimension. It took a call of a Frost scion to my office that ended up alerting both of us to this issue."

"What's going on, Strike? Tell it to us straight," Rumble, the oldest scion of Donner, called out.

"Krieg, reveal the map on the main screens," Strike said.

Krieg moved his hands over the consoles and spread the world map across all three screens for the greatest detail.

"Every single red dot is a beacon alert over the past five years. Each alert corresponds to a Frost scion or their crystal partner in danger," Strike said. "Every single alert—" He shook his head. "Let me repeat that." He made a slow half-circle movement to address everything. "Every. Single. Alert." With those words, he studied the entire group. "These alerts were either ignored, noted and put aside, or crossed off without being investigated."

There were quiet murmurings throughout the crowds. Some shuffled their feet in place. No one spoke up against the accusation.

"How do you know this?" Kringle asked.

"I will let Krieg explain about the database," Strike said.

"Every single beacon alert creates an automatic record in the database, sir. Each agent or staff member opens the record to read the details about the record and must investigate it. The individual log-in is recorded with a time and date stamp and what they did." Krieg flashed up about five different records from different CPD offices. "There's the initial information created by the beacon." He highlighted the areas with his mouse movements. "Then this is the first opening of the records by each office." He moved to a different section. "With the log-ins specific to agent or staff. And the last part is where notes were either added or the record closed without further investigation and filed."

"Thank you for that explanation. What happened with these cases?"

Krieg moved to the last section. "As you can view here, there are no notes filled in or attached. This happens in all thirty-eight cases. Each beacon alert corresponds to a specific Frost scion and their partner, though a couple of them are repetitive. This is an example of one of them. This beacon in Boston recorded two different alerts regarding Frost scion, Jacob Serac, and his partner. One was the initial beacon three years ago and the second this morning. This morning according to mortal EST time, not the Dimension."

"This morning's alert?" Kringle asked. "What happened this morning?"

"My Frost dimension protected cabin was attacked," Jacob said.

Kringle stepped to the center of the room and assessed the crowd. "Explain this. Why were these alerts ignored and closed without investigation?"

"Usual protocol regarding Frosts. We don't involve the CPD in their business," someone said.

The rest of the crowd nodded and murmured similar responses.

"Why?"

"They're Frosts," a group said together.

"They don't bother us. We don't talk to them," someone else added.

"Which needs to change now," an icy tone said in a booming tone. A tornado of wind, snow, and ice swirled within the center of the room. It dissipated to reveal a foreboding slender figure over eight-feet tall.

"And here's my boss and grandfather," Jacob muttered.

"He knows how to make an entrance," Strike said.

"Never fails in that," Jacob said. "Probably perfected it over the centuries to master the great entrance."

"Greetings and welcome to our gathering, Jokul," Kringle said.

Jokul Frosti nodded toward Kringle and stepped closer through the crowd to stand near Kringle.

"Pardon me, Lord Frosti, greetings. I would like to ask something and continue this discussion about the missed alerts," Rumble said while he pushed forward through the crowd.

After a glance at Kringle and Frosti, Strike nodded. "Go ahead, Rumble."

"Other than the alerts having to do with the Frosts, why bring up this issue? What happened to these Frosts to cause the alerts with them and their partners? Why call an all-alert meeting for some missed alerts?" Rumble asked. "Is something else happening with these alerts than an issue with our protocols?"

"Our fellow NPD brethren and their partners are being attacked. Everyone had damage done to them or their partners," Strike said.

"By whom?"

"We believe the Yule Lads and their mother, the sorceress Grýla, are behind the attacks. This could be done to weaken Jokul Frosti and the barrier surrounding the NPD and the beacon crystal," Strike said.

"What proof do you have? Other than all these alerts," someone asked.

"Me. This attack happened to my crystal partner and myself," Jacob said while he stepped forward. "I am Jacob Serac, direct grandson of Jokul Frosti and the son of the European Jack Frost. I am the Frost scion of the American East Coast and my territory stretches from Greenland down to the Carolinas and inward to the Great Lakes and the Mississippi River. At this moment, I might be the oldest Frost standing in front of you and not in ice sleep."

"What happened to you?" Rumble asked.

"One of the Lads used a dark spell upon my partner and clouded my crystal heart," Jacob said. "If I hadn't caught what was happening, our connection would have been severed and I would be sent to an ice sleep."

"Crystal heart? Spell?"

There were other confused murmurings.

"Why does this warrant an all-call alert? We always deal with the Lads and nothing happens to the barrier," Rumble said.

Others called out their agreements and mumblings about being pulled away from their locations.

"Let's get out of here. This isn't worth our time," some of the reindeer and elves said.

More agreed with them.

When they tried to activate portals, nothing happened.

"What's happening—"

"My portal isn't connecting—"

"No one is to leave," Kringle said. "All portals are disconnected."

Strike studied the annoyed crowd. Then he turned to Jacob. "They don't understand the significance. They're focusing on the minor issues and not the overall problem. I don't know how to explain—" he muttered and broke off. He paced a few quick steps from Krieg's spot to where Jacob stood.

"Unlike them, you know what it all means because of our talks," Jacob said.

"Perhaps a demonstration and explanation of Frosts is in order, Grandson," Jokul said in his wintry voice that cut through like ice. He stepped forward. His tall, thin figure cloaked in a magnificent heavy cloak that resembled the blackest ice to the midnight sky and decorated in filigree layers of frost and ice. Then he held out one long-fingered hand, his skin tinged blueish-white. "Your heart, please."

"It will reveal our secrets," Jacob said.

"It is time to reveal them. Most of them," Jokul said. "Far past time. Or this impending disaster would never have occurred."

Pulling his heart from a pocket, Jacob enlarged it with his magic. "The spell is no longer there."

"I can reverse the time upon the heart to reveal what happened without causing damage. Trust me to take care of your heart, my grandson."

Jacob placed his heart in his grandfather's hand.

Jokul moved toward the center. He snapped his fingers and a bright spotlight appeared within the middle. With a gesture, everyone else moved back.

"I will offer a brief explanation to help everyone understand the significance behind the findings and the alerts. The reasons why all of you were called here by Strike and my grandson. There isn't much time, so this will be a brief one," Jokul said. "Upon a Frost scion's genes activating to transform them from mortal to a Frost, they slip into a brief ice sleep while their body changes. Upon rising, the first thing a Frost must learn is how to create a crystal heart from the magical ice crystals formed around and through their actual heart. These ice crystals are the vital pieces of a Frost's magic and abilities. To survive, they must remove the ice and create a crystal heart.

"The heart contains a piece of their vitality, life, and magic. To protect this heart and prevent them from turning dark, they entrust their crystal heart to a life partner. Often their heart will take the form of a pendant, a ring, or a pin. Their partner carries the heart throughout their lifetime, protecting their Frost, but preventing them from turning to ice, forgetting their position, and vital connection to the circle of life.

"If this does not happen between a Frost and their partner, the heart cracks. It could shatter if the relationship and trust isn't repaired. Once shattered, the ice reforms around the Frost's heart. This process sends them to an ancient shelter I created to protect them while they slip into a deep ice sleep. For now, this ancient shelter location remains a secret among the Frosts for they remain vulnerable while trapped in this sleep. The sleep can last from a decade to a century or more depending on what happened and their status. Upon wakening, the cycle begins again for the Frost with the creation of a new heart. A Frost's life, power, and status begins and ends with their crystal heart.

"Does everyone understand?" Jokul studied the crowd. When there were no rumblings, he enlarged Jacob's heart and threw it up toward the light where it remained hovering. The light poured through the crystal and revealed the faint cracks created by the dark spell and the rift between Jacob and Devyn. "There are multiple stages of failure for a crystal heart. This heart reveals minor cracks. I would put it at a Stage Two. Stage Five is a complete shatter. Now, if we turn back time a few hours—" Jokul spun the heart counter-clockwise with a burst of magic.

When the heart slowed, dark dangerous clouds shadowed the entire crystal complex. Deeper cracks went through the structure.

Sounds of concern and awe moved through the crowd.

"This is a Stage Four. Almost imminent shattering if the situation didn't improve. Being of a certain age and strength, Jacob understood what was happening and went through the procedures to heal his relationship with his crystal partner," Jokul said.

"What caused the shadows?" Rumble asked.

"A very dangerous spell," Strike said. "It was placed upon a gold watch and gifted to Jacob's crystal partner about three years ago when he catapulted into a more prestigious position at his workplace. The person who gave him the watch was called Victor Merrowynd."

More murmurs and conversation happened at the name.

"One of the Yule Lads," Rumble said.

"That was our guess after a thorough conversation with Jacob's crystal partner. They placed this spell within the watch and convinced Jacob's partner to always carry it, perhaps due to a compulsion enchantment. This allowed the spell to take hold of him and infect the crystal heart he also wore. This combination caused the shadow clouds and the cracks," Strike said.

"Why didn't you shatter?" Rumble asked Jacob.

"Possibly due to my age and strength. This isn't my first crystal heart," Jacob said. "Though, I now believe it didn't take immediate effect because we learned my partner is part-Cheimon. One of the first crystal heart partners of the bloodlines, I believe." He looked to Jokul for confirmation, who nodded. "If that is true, it could be a benefit for all future crystal heart partners to carry some Cheimon blood when they accept the heart. It would strengthen them, the relationship, and, in turn, the Frost."

"That is for another discussion," Jokul said.

"Of course," Jacob said. "Plus, a look at the archives with the historian elves."

"To connect all of this back to our main issue with the alerts, Jacob called me in to assist with a different problem which is when we discovered his partner's Cheimon blood," Strike said to pick up the conversation. "Another conversation led us to the discovery of the spell. I was able to recover the spell from the watch into a special retrieval globe and sent it to the R&D department for analysis. Though, I knew the flavor of the darkness held the Lads' touch."

"You think all of these other alerts are caused by this spell thing on either the Frost or their partner?" Rumble asked.

"Yes, but there is some research—" Strike looked to Jokul and Jacob.

"There is a place where we can search for the spell. We'll need some trained retrieval specialists and protective globes," Jacob said.

"Consider it done," Kringle called out.

"Though, we believe this is the answer to all the alerts and it's causing more trouble than anyone could imagine," Strike said.

"Why?" Rumble asked.

"Master Jokul, how many Frosts are active to support you and the beacon's magic?" Strike asked.

"Counting Jacob, there are twenty-two," Jokul said. "The rest are in ice sleep. Our numbers were low to begin, but this spell disease crippled our numbers. The FVI are working overtime to make up the differences." He recalled the crystal heart, minimized it, and returned it to Jacob.

Jacob slipped the crystal back into a protective inner pocket of his coat.

"And your strength? An honest answer, my Lord," Rumble said.

"Considering my age, I'm holding up and will be replenished with the Winter Solstice," Jokul said. "If I'm unable to replenish, the barrier will weaken. Kringle and Mother Nature can't maintain the barrier's strength without me."

"And this is the potential dilemma and disaster awaiting us. The Winter Solstice is when the beacon, the barrier, and our magic is replenished. Our most sacred day. Our most vulnerable day," Strike said.

"Do you expect the Lads to stage an attack?" someone else asked before Rumble could.

"They attacked my cabin with a specialized needle designed to hit and injure my crystal partner," Jacob said. "It's why I'm here in the NPD with my partner instead of in the mortal world performing my Frost duties."

Loud mutterings and grumbles rose at Jacob's words.

"Does everyone understand why I put out the all-call alert? Because of our negligence in our duties to all NPD residents and bloodlines, the Lads found a hole in our defenses and are using it against us. They are poised to attack our barriers and home on the Winter Solstice. Two days, everyone. I repeat. In two days' time, we could lose everything we hold dear," Strike said.

"Tell us what you need," Rumble called out.

"Here is the plan..." Strike began to lay out the beginnings of the plan he fiddled with while at the Boston office.

Chapter Nine

When Strike reached the point in the meeting where they no longer needed Jacob and Jokul Frosti, the reindeer released them from the group. Jacob handed over the needle for Strike to bring it to R&D for investigation and research. They promised to keep in contact, especially when they reached the Cavern and needed the retrieval specialists to capture the spells.

Jokul led the way out of the CPD headquarters and back to the street. Instead of creating his version of a portal to the Cavern, he walked toward the building in progress. When they drew closer, he stopped and studied the construction.

"Grandfather?" Jacob stopped next to him. He glanced at the building and back to his powerful, often imposing grandfather.

"What do you think of this construction? The progress is coming along. Another two weeks and the structure will be completed. Then the interior will be considered, but that will move along with speed. These elves know what they're doing, even with a Frost forming the building."

"Are they using your magic?"

"Hmm. I imbued the entire ground and materials with my magic. The building will be sentient and reactive for all Frosts and FVI members."

"Does this mean that you intend this for the Frosts?"

"Yes, Grandson, I believe now is the time to change the way we control and organize our business."

"How do you want to change it?"

"Time to change everything. We should move our organization to a centralized headquarters like the CPD. I want to rearrange everything and consolidate the Frosts and their partners. When the winter events happen, the central headquarters will send FVI agents first to assess the event. Once they send back a report, a Frost will be dispatched to organize the on-site response."

"Which is completely different then what we are doing now."

"Everyone on their own. Separated. Isolated."

"Vulnerable to attack," Jacob said.

"Exactly, Grandson. This is one of the reasons why the Lads were able to attack the Frosts and their partners with little to no response from anyone. I didn't know of the issue with the CPD and their non-response to our distress alerts. That bothered me greatly when I listened," Jokul said. He shook his head deep within the hood. Then he paced a few times. A few swirls of snow rose around his feet that grew with his anger. "Kringle and I will speak about that later. Both of us will make sure the agents and support staff follow the changes to the procedures."

"I'm sure Strike will also follow through."

"He seems quite competent. I'm grateful you made the decision to contact him."

"He was the only one I considered contacting when Devyn reacted weird to the R&D concoction."

"How is your Devyn?"

"I left him with the Head Tinkerer discovering the mysteries of the watch the Lads gave him. With the removal of the spell and telling him the truth, our connection is growing stronger."

"I recognized the healing within the heart. Truth is stronger than anything. You have always been my strongest Frost scion. One I can always rely upon for anything, no matter where you went," Jokul said.

Jacob turned to look upon his grandfather. "What do you need from me?"

"I would like for you to remain within the NPD and run the headquarters. The other Frosts and FVI will listen and follow you. Now that we know your partner is Cheimon, he can remain here with you."

"The other Frosts though don't have the same connection with their partners. They can't leave their partners for multiple seasons."

"The current ones in the mortal realm will need to remain where they are. For the Frosts in the ice sleep and future ones, I believe we can search for Cheimon-blood crystal partners to connect. I will instruct all the Jack Frosts to search from Cheimon-blood females to bear new scions. Most modern mortal females no longer wish to bear a stranger's child unless there are underlying issues. Modernity changes everything for us and we must learn to adjust."

"Multiple changes."

"A necessary problem for everyone to face."

Though Jokul's face and gaze were hidden deep within the cowl, Jacob knew his grandfather studied him.

"Take some time to think about the offer. Speak with your partner. This is a life-changing event."

"He'll want to know if we can leave at times, visit Boston and our friends."

"Yes, you'll be able to leave for vacations. At least, you do not have to worry about flights and connections."

Jacob laughed. He couldn't believe the ancient immortal made a joke.

"Come. Let us travel to the Cavern. There are more pressing matters." Jokul waved a hand and created a tornado of blue magic, ice, and snow. This was his version of a snow globe portal.

Controlling his laughter, Jacob placed his hand on Jokul's arm and stepped through the portal with him.

They reappeared in the welcome area of the ancient Ice Cavern. A specialized cave built deep inside a dormant Artic volcano by Jokul Frosti and imbued with special magic and power. The cave remained hidden from all electronics. The entire volcano system remained firmly in the Dimension, while a simple mountain stood in its place in the mortal realm with no value to provoke further investigation by any Artic explores or satellites.

Jacob rolled his shoulders upon stepping into the welcome area. It felt different being here while awake and not after an extended sleep. A collection of specially trained FVI agents protected the entire cavern and the precious inhabitants.

"Greetings and welcome, Lord Frosti. Lord Jacob, greetings and welcome to the Cavern. I'm FVI Agent Lucia, the current Head Guardian of the Cavern," Lucia, a white-haired elf, said. She wore the typical Cavern outfit of a heavy midnight blue coat with snowy fur, dark leggings, and soft boots. She wore fingerless gloves to help combat the cold while still able to perform her duties.

Jokul made sure the Cavern maintained a constant temperature that hovered above freezing, but remained comfortable for the living. Only the increased amount of sleeping scions dropped the temperature.

Even Jacob felt the change in the atmosphere.

"Greetings, Lucia. How is everything?" Jacob asked.

"Quite crowded. We are having trouble maintaining the temperatures in the rest of the cavern," Lucia admitted.

"I can sense the change. What is happening?" Jokul asked.

"I apologize, Lord Frosti, but it has been so cold. Even for us." Lucia shook her head and tried to hide the tears appearing at her eyes. "It got so bad that only three agents remained on duty for each shift. The rest of us remain within the living quarters with the fireplaces running and warm cider and cocoa in our bellies. I sent messages, but not sure if they went through."

"Messages?" Jokul turned to face Lucia. He pushed back the cowl. "I never received anything. How did you send them?"

"Through the normal channels, my Lord. The CPD Headquarters with your attention. I sent six messages about the conditions and increased numbers," Lucia said. "I was about to portal one of us to CPD to personally locate you and bring you here."

"Something has happened with the channels. Why would they be blocked?" Jokul looked around. Snow swirled around him. He held out his hands and fingers to send out tendrils of magic throughout the cavern.

"Grandfather..." Jacob said.

Jokul closed one of his hands into a fist. "Eirlys Minstix, come to me now," he called out in a hollow frozen tone.

Jacob and Lucia visibly shuddered and shivered at the sudden drop in temperature around them.

A small dark-haired female elf walked out of the back hallway from the living quarters. There was a glowing necklace against the dark coat. Jokul's magic swirled around the necklace while he compelled her to move toward him.

"The necklace," Jacob said.

"Is it the same spell?" Jokul asked. His tone a touch warmer, but he didn't release the elf girl from his control.

Jacob held out a hand and sent his own magic. The same flash of darkness that haunted Devyn's watch responded to him. "Yes. The same spell."

"Who gave you the necklace, Eirlys?" Jokul asked.

"My boyfriend. Isn't it beautiful? I met him during my summer vacation. It was a fantasy meeting coming true. I found my perfect man, strong, handsome, and he adores me," Eirlys said. Her voice soft and not quite there. Her gaze was distant.

"What is his name?" Jacob asked.

"Victor. Victor Merrowynd. I think he'll ask me to marry him at Winter Solstice," Eirlys said.

"Will he be there?"

"As my date and escort. I requested the night because I have been here the longest after Lucia. I will dance with Victor under the Solstice's energy, drink ice wine, and accept his proposal," Eirlys said. "Then he will take me away from here. Forever. No more ice and loneliness." A dreamy smile curled her lips.

"Same spell, different results," Jacob said. "It's the same man who gave Devyn the watch."

"Did Victor tell you to block the messages Lucia sent?" Jokul asked.

"Of course. Nothing is wrong here. The Frosts will sleep. We slave over a bunch of icicles with no respect, thanks, or financial recompense." Eirlys' face twisted with hate. "Why should I care about them?"

"It has been your position for over fifty years. It's an honor and a privilege to serve Lord Frosti and the Frosts," Lucia snapped. "Stupid, stupid girl. How dare you say this about our sacred duty."

"Stupid Lucia for doing nothing more than sending a stupid message. Always bowing and following the—"

Jokul snapped his fingers and a layer of frost covered Eirlys' mouth to cut her off. "Is this her normal behavior and thoughts? Or is she influenced by the spell."

"The R&D will need to investigate. Her and the necklace. Either way, she can't remain here or be at the event," Jacob said. "Unless we use her as bait or a lure for Merrowynd."

"Where is her room?" Jokul asked Lucia.

"Next to mine."

"Search it. You will find the messages. Perhaps letters to Victor. Bring everything you find to me. Everything will be considered as evidence for her actions and behavior before and after the necklace incident. Punishment for her betrayal and actions will be considered after the investigation and removal of the spell," Jokul said. "I need to visit the Frosts. I will make sure the temperature is readjusted. You should know that the hearts were shattered under unnatural means, Lucia. They should not be here."

"Oh, sweet icicles, I wondered why so many were appearing," Lucia said. "We never had so many scions sleep within a ten-year period. Two or three appeared every night. Can you awaken them?"

"I must review all of their hearts to confirm our suspicions. If this is the case, then yes, they will be awakened and taken to their homes on Frost Ridge to recover. Things should regulate, but if more scions appear. Contact me through this," Jokul said. With a wave of his hand, he created a frozen snowflake on a chain. He placed the chain around Lucia's neck. "Hold it in your hand. Call my name. I will hear you and respond. This will work until we can repair everything."

"Thank you, Lord Frosti." Lucia touched the snowflake and smiled. "I will go search the room and gather the others to assist." She hurried off to complete Jokul's task.

"Let's find the Wall of Hearts," Jokul said.

Lucia pointed to her former co-worker. "What about her?"

"She isn't going to move or speak until I free her," Jokul said. "Into a cell deep within Ice Ridge Prison for her assistance in hurting all of the Frosts." He went to touch the necklace.

"No, wait!" Jacob shouted.

Jokul stopped inches from the necklace. He looked upon his grandson.

"Don't touch it, Grandfather. The spell might attach to you. The special retrieval elves will secure her and it for us."

"Very well. I will leave it for them."

"I promise they will retrieve it with care. And her. If that is what the R&D and investigators determine, she will be tried by the courts and sent to Ice Ridge. Let's go to the Frosts. They need us first," Jacob said.

With a nod, Jokul glared at the elf. "Go stand in the corner. Do not move until I command."

Under his full control, the elf grimaced, tried to complain and fight back to comply with the necklace's compulsion spell, but followed his command.

With the traitor under Jokul's command and out of the way, they passed through the hallway toward the massive central room of the Ice Cavern. It lengthened and shortened based upon the amount of sleeping scions. Each shattered Frost rested upon an ice bed. A dome of protective ice and frost covered each Frost. Their name inscribed upon the ice. The Cavern was at its longest length in recorded history.

Jacob moved through the beds and stopped at one bed. "Darío." The Spanish born and stationed Frost slept underneath the dome. He touched the ice. "We're here, Darío, we're here. You're not alone. None of you are alone. We discovered what is happening to us and we'll fight back. That I swear upon our oaths as Frosts." Then he followed Jokul to the massive wall of small compartments.

This was the magical Wall of Hearts that protected all of the crystals. Each compartment closed by a frosted ice door. Inside, gathered within a silver dish, were the shattered remains of a crystal heart. Upon each frosted door was the inscribed name and date of the Frost.

Jacob glanced down a few columns and discovered his previous shattered hearts. It was quite strange to see his name upon the doors and how long he's been awake since the last shattering.

With a wave of Jokul's hands, the doors open for each Frost under suspicion of being impacted by the Lads' spells. He called all hearts forward. The pieces spun in the air in front of the compartments. Then he ordered the pieces to rebuild each heart. When each heart spun in its place, he reversed the time upon each heart until the tell-tale dark shadows appeared.

Jacob gasped in utter horror at the darkness spread before him. "Proof of the spell."

"In every single heart," Jokul said. "Contact the retrieval agents. Now."

"We don't know where the spell originated. We'll have to track and evaluate each Frost." Jacob pulled out the globe Strike gave him. He spoke the words and tossed it into a corner.

The tell-tale swirl of blue and snowflakes spun to open the portal.

Seven retrieval elf agents from R&D stepped through and bowed to them.

"Greetings, Lord Frosti, Lord Jacob. Thank you for the honor of receiving our assistance in this matter. I am the head retrieval elf, Alabaster Everdancer," Alabaster said with another bow. "These are my associates."

"Welcome to the Ice Cavern, home of the sleeping Frosts. What you see here is considered sacred and secret. No one is to speak or write about anything they discover here. Once you leave by portal, you will be unable to find your way back. Only Frosts and those agents assigned to their care know the location," Jokul said.

"Understood and we offer our sacred oath to protect the secrets of the Frosts," Alabaster said.

"Take over control, grandson," Jokul said.

"Here are the shattered hearts of the Frosts," Jacob said. "They are all sleeping within the great chamber. Lord Frosti reversed the time upon each Frost's heart to the point the spell appeared within the crystal. Though we do not know the origins of the spell."

"From the investigation of your crystal partner's spell, it can only be attached to an item and given to the mortal partner. Only then will the spell infect the connected Frost," Alabaster said.

"Then we'll have to track down all the partners, portal to their location, and search for the object and spell. The head keeper, Lucia, should have the necessary records," Jacob said. "There is another issue."

"What is that, Lord Jacob?"

"We discovered one of the elves has been infected by a spelled necklace. It was given to her by the same Lad who gave my partner his watch. She interfered with the operations and communications of the Cavern."

"Where is this elf now?" Alabaster turned to another elf. "Mint Plumbow, follow Lord Jacob and me to collect this elf. The rest will remain here. Prepare for the retrieval of the spells."

A younger elf stepped forward to separate from the small group.

Jacob glanced to Jokul, who nodded, and led them back through to the welcome area. He pointed to the elf in the corner. "Right now, she is under Jokul's magic. Frost covers her mouth and controls her movement. That will dissipate when she is out of his reach."

"Lord Jacob, Fir and Elm assisted me. We discovered everything Lord Frosti requested from Eirlys' room. Perhaps a little bit more than even I expected. There are a series of diaries. She despised being here, but couldn't get a transfer, no matter how many times she tried to move," Lucia said when she entered the room from the back hallway. She carried a bright red envelope that was thick and heavy.

"Thank you, Lucia, I'm sorry to hear she's been so unhappy watching over us. Was there anything in particular?"

"The location. The hours. The financial payment. The distance from her family. She complained about everything."

"Should I ask the Council to send investigators to speak with the rest of elves about their positions here? I know Master Jokul is planning on altering things with the Frosts, perhaps we could also focus on the Cavern and its caretakers."

Lucia rubbed her hands together in a worried fashion.

"Lucia?"

"Yes, please, that would be helpful. Now I worry about all the others."

"I will make it happen."

"Thank you, Lord Jacob, thank you."

"Do not worry, Lucia, I promise you'll not be forgotten or left alone. Never again," Jacob said. He moved to Lucia to stand in front of her and lowered his voice to keep the conversation between them. "What you do is sacred and important. Without you and the other caretakers, the sleeping Frosts are extremely vulnerable. Both in sleep and upon awakening without a crystal, we're assailable and defenseless. You and the caretakers know this and watch over us. I'll make sure all of you are rewarded and compensated."

"Thank you, Lord Jacob," Lucia said.

With a nod, Jacob stepped back. "Please hand the package to the elf, Mint. He will take it along with Eirlys back to the headquarters."

When Lucia handed over the red envelope, Mint tucked it into his bag. Then he pulled out a pair of special ice cuffs and locked them around Eirlys' wrists. "Do I portal her to R&D under full watch?"

"Correct. Make sure to retrieve the necklace under full protection and place her in a warded cell until the investigation is done," Alabaster said.

"Should I return to help complete the rest of the task?"

"No, this is your priority. The female elf and necklace. Investigate everything possible and connect it back to the original spell on the watch. This is a spell upon an elf, not a mortal, so expect the differences and search for them."

"Understood, Alabaster, I'll report my findings to Agent Strike," Mint said. He pulled out a globe, spoke into it, and tossed it to the side. He grabbed Eirlys' arm, dragged her through the portal, and disappeared.

"Any other issues?" Alabaster asked.

"That's the unexpected one. The rest... well, that's based on what we find with the sleeping Frosts," Jacob said. "Lucia, one more thing. Could you please locate the records of the impacted Frosts and their recent crystal partner?"

"Of course, sir, may I ask why?"

"We'll need the names and locations of each partner to retrieve the infected object and clear them of the spell. They could still be in trouble and under the spell's influence if they continue to hold the object."

"I will search the records with Elm and Fir. I continue to trust both of them. After creating a list, I will meet you back in the cavern," Lucia said.

"Thank you." With that part covered, Jacob led Alabaster back into the main cavern.

"I happened to notice the temperature is quite cold. Far colder than anything within the Center or the numerous buildings. Is it normally this cold?"

"No, I believe it's due to the influx of Frosts within their ice domes. Lord Frosti will check into the atmospheric conditions. He is the only one who can alter anything within the Cavern."

"Understood."

"Will the temperature interfere with your work?"

"No, but we will make adjustments if necessary."

When they reached the entrance to the great chamber, they stopped to study the massive cavern. At some point, Jokul shifted the spinning hearts' positions. Each heart hovered over a specific Frost within the cavern to guide the retrieval specialists.

"This should make locating the origins a little easier," Jokul said.

"Excellent suggestion, sir. Elves, go to a heart and begin the investigation and retrieval," Alabaster ordered.

"We usually call them crystals," Jacob said. "It doesn't matter though."

"Crystals. We'll take care of the crystals and the sleeping Frosts. No further harm will come to them," Alabaster said. "My solemn oath upon the Beacon."

The remaining elves swore the same oath.

"Grateful for your care of my children," Jokul said.

With the Spirit of Winter's acceptance and approval, the elves selected a column of beds and went to work.

Jokul moved about the room to spin a heart to help assist in locating the origin and timing. With his magic and skill, they were able to recall the object given to the crystal partner by the Lads. The elves made notes on everything and used the special globes to retrieve the dangerous spells.

When they reached Darío's bed, Jacob moved to check the progress.

"The records you requested, Lord Jacob," Lucia said and handed him a dark green folder. "How is the retrieval coming along?"

"Thank you, Lucia. Slow progress, but we're recovering the spells and locating the objects that are the root cause of each shattering." Jacob flipped through the records until he found Darío's page.

"The spell remains here, Lord Jacob. The object is held within the Frost's hand," Alabaster said.

"What? How is that possible?" Jacob asked.

Jokul flowed through the aisles until he reached them. With a wave of his hand, he dispelled the ice dome. Then he loosened the ice around Darío's hand.

Jacob set aside the folder and opened Darío's fingers. "A ring. It's a ring." He checked the paper. "The ring isn't from him, but according to this sheet, his crystal partner of thirty-five years, Emelina Del Bosque, threw it at him and cursed at him. This final event caused his crystal to shatter. A beacon alert went through the Madrid office two years prior to the shattering. After the initial check, it was never investigated."

"That ring holds the spell," Alabaster said. He collected a small retrieval globe and used it to pull the spell from the ring and Darío's frozen body. While he retrieved the spell, the shadows within the heart disappeared. Then he collected and secured the ring. "There. All clean."

"Thirty-seven years with Emelina. He'll want to return to her, if possible. They have three children, two sons and a daughter. The youngest is sixteen. All three children show the signs of becoming future Frosts. Emelina will need to be cleansed. Some explanation will need to be created to support what happened," Jacob said. He glanced to Jokul.

"We will awaken and assist him in returning to her. Along with a retrieval agent to cleanse her of any lingering spell before he offers her a new crystal. I will have her and the children check for Cheimon blood and the Frost genetics. They were a strong pair, able to secure most of the European territory," Jokul said.

Hours later, they reached the final bed with Alabaster.

"This is the last Frost and spell," Alabaster said when he labeled and secured the globe.

Jacob made notes in the folder. "Please use these notes to locate all of the crystal partners and recover the object and spell."

"Should we ask if they wish to see their Frost again?"

"Yes, please be careful and don't mention them being a Frost. Most crystal partners know nothing about Frosts and the Cheimon. I starred the crystal partners that know the truth about the Cheimon. Darío's partner is one of them," Jacob said. He held out the folder.

"We'll take care with all of them. If they want nothing to do with the Frosts, the R&D have a special concoction that can remove the necessary memories. They'll not remember our visit or the object," Alabaster said. "We must drop off the globes first to get them processed, collect more globes and items, then head back out."

"Thank you for your assistance and care. Here is a quicker portal directly into R&D," Jokul said. He swirled his hand to create one of his portals.

"You're welcome. We'll make sure you're kept updated about the progress with the crystal partners," Alabaster said. "Elves. To me. Through the portal."

With those orders, the five elves bowed to Jokul and Jacob. Then they stepped through the portal and disappeared. With a final bow of respect, Alabaster slipped through the portal.

Jokul closed it. Then he turned to face the great room. With a wave of his hands, he returned the clear crystals back to their compartments and closed the doors. "Time to wake our brethren." Calling upon his magic, Jokul removed the ice domes from the specific Frosts. Then he carefully began the defrost each Frost, careful not to place them in shock.

One at a time, each scion opened their eyes.

Lucia and the other caretakers stepped into the room. They spread out and covered each waking Frost in a blanket, offered special tea and cookies to assist in the recovery, and supported them.

While this process happened, Jacob felt something vibrate within his inner jacket pocket. He pulled out the thin ice tablet and touched the screen.

First there was a message from Mistletoe. The FVI elves and fairies cleaned up his Boston cabin, repacked their suitcases, and cleaned out the perishables in the fridge and freezer. They portaled everything to the house and Mistle arranged everything and cleaned up. The FVI members returned to Boston and pulled in additional teams to cover the rest of the winter events happening in Jacob's absence. The head FVI member, Aspen — a very lovely and considerate elf according to Mistle's additional note — also gathered the paperwork from the Boston cabin's desk into a folder and hand-delivered it to Mistletoe, who left it on Jacob's desk.

After the extended message from Mistletoe, a new message from the Head Tinkerer, Rusty, appeared. Jacob read the message, hoped things went well back at the workshop.

"Rusty and Devyn discovered the hidden locator device. Rusty captured it within a globe, but Devyn doesn't want him to send it to headquarters. He wants to bring it there with me," Jacob said. He tapped out a reply and slid the tablet back into the pocket.

"Go to him."

"What?"

Jokul moved to Jacob. "Go and spend time with your crystal partner. Discuss my proposal with him."

"I should be here. For my brothers."

"The recovery will take time because this is an unusual situation from the shattering to the wakening. I must explain everything to them. Once stabilized, I will move them to their Frost Ridge homes with a special caretaker assigned to them for a couple of days. Then we'll work on creating new crystals. If possible, I can help them reconnect to their partners or locate a new one," Jokul said.

"If you need assistance—"

"I will contact you, my grandson. For now, I need you on the battlefield and within the active investigation with Agent Strike."

"Regarding the caretakers—"

"I heard your conversation with Lucia. I will add them to the plans for the new central headquarters."

Jacob nodded.

"Shall I send you back to the Workshop?"

"Please."

With a smile, Jokul created a new portal. "Say hello to your crystal partner. I look forward to meeting him at the Winter Solstice."

"Thank you, Grandfather," Jacob said and moved to the portal.

"Thank you, Grandson, for figuring out what was happening," Jokul said before Jacob stepped through the portal.

Chapter Ten

Thanks to Jokul's portal, Jacob stepped out in front of the Tinkerer HQ. Immediately, he noticed the difference from when he left for the Cavern. Nutcrackers armed with forever ice swords patrolled the streets with a team of four Toy Soldiers.

"Quicker than I expected," he muttered and headed toward the Tinkerer HQ main doors.

A pair of Toy Soldiers stopped him. "Please halt. State your name and business," one demanded.

"Jacob Serac, Frost scion of America NE. My crystal partner, Devyn, is with the Head Tinkerer, Rusty Magicmoon. I'm here to pick him up," Jacob said.

One of the Toy Soldiers used an ice tablet to check Jacob's information. "He's approved for entrance by the Head Tinkerer."

The second Toy Soldier stepped aside and opened the door for Jacob. "Welcome to the Tinkerer HQ, Lord Serac."

"Thank you. New orders from CPD and Lord Kringle?" Jacob asked.

"Yes, sir. A potential attack may be looming and we're here to make sure things are secure and safe for everyone," the soldier said.

"Great. Thank you," Jacob said and disappeared inside the building. Then he moved down the halls back to the Head Tinkerer's office.

At the administrative desk, Starlight remained behind her desk. She wasn't quite as cheery as she was during his earlier visit.

"Greetings, Starlight," Jacob said.

"Oh, Lord Jacob!" Starlight jumped in her chair. A frail hand pressed to her chest. Her eyes went wide from the quick scare. "Cookie crumbles!"

"I apologize."

"I have been on edge all afternoon. Such cookie crumbles with all this scare and security. What could be happening? All they said was to watch what we do, say, and mention if we sense any dark magic," Starlight said.

"Trust in the Nutcrackers and the Toy Soldiers. They know what to do and will make sure you're safe," Jacob said.

"Yes. Yes. Of course. Trust in them. Let me announce you." Starlight got up and went to the door. She opened one of the double doors and leaned inside. "Rusty, Lord Jacob is here."

"Send him on in," Rusty's deep voice called back.

Starlight smiled at him. "Would you like anything to drink or eat?"

"No, but thank you. I plan on taking Devyn out to eat unless my house elf created something for our evening meal," Jacob said and walked through the door. He closed it behind him. Then he headed deeper into the cavernous room.

Located in the far back, he found his crystal partner hunched over a table with the Head Tinkerer. Parts, gears, tools, and pieces spread around them. A project building and rising between them.

"Greetings, Devyn, Rusty," Jacob said.

"Jacob!" Devyn called out when he looked up. He removed the magnifying glasses, dropped them on the table, and darted over to Jacob.

Opening his arms, Jacob accepted an armful of Devyn. He felt as Devyn wrapped his arms tight around his waist and almost squeeze the breath out of him. Then he felt the slight tremors move through Devyn's body.

"Devyn, love, what is wrong?"

"Armed soldiers moved through the building, went to the door, but something stopped them. They hollered until Rusty opened the door and explained everything. The soldiers had orders from something called CPD to check every room. This truly makes it real. What is happening to us? To this place. Isn't it?" Devyn asked, when he pulled back to look at Jacob.

Jacob nodded. "It's getting real to everyone since I went to CPD with Strike and spoke to everyone, including Lord Kringle and my grandfather, the Spirit of Winter. The soldiers are called Toy Soldiers with Nutcracker officers."

"CPD?"

"Cheimon Patrol Division. It's where Strike and Krieg work. I'll explain more later if you want to understand everything."

"Okay."

Jacob stepped back and rubbed his hands up and down Devyn's arms to calm him. "How did you come along with your little project?"

"Oh. Oh! Yes, we found it." Devyn pulled away and raced back to the table. He carefully collected a small globe and brought it back. "There's the device. A transmitter of some type like I expected. It was hidden within the gears, not interfering with the works. They switched the transmitter with a real piece so that the movement allowed an energy to pulse it to send out the signal. Obviously, it's not supposed to be there. Rusty felt the magic pulsing from it. He captured it inside this globe for safe transport."

"Good work, both of you. What about the watch?"

"We put the watch back together and replaced the piece with something else. Rusty colored it a bright red so anyone who investigates how the transmitter worked can see where it was originally placed. Either way, I don't want to keep it. I would like someone else to take it. It no longer has any special meaning to me. Now that I know the true story behind it and what it did to us."

Jacob gathered the globe in one hand and lifted it to check out the tiny device hovering within the middle. "Interesting little thing. This could track your whereabouts even through my Frost dimension shields."

"Supposedly, but that's up to the R&D investigation in how it all works," Devyn said. "Rusty didn't want me to touch it."

"I wouldn't want you to touch anything created by the Lads. We can leave the watch with the CPD or R&D if that is your preference." Jacob handed it back to Devyn. "Do you want to carry this to R&D?"

"Please. I would like to see this project through all the way."

"Of course."

With a nod, Devyn returned to collect the watch and slid it in a pocket. Then he found where he stashed his coat and pulled that back on. "Thank you so much for teaching me about everything, Rusty. I hope we can get together again."

"You're welcome any time in my office and my department," Rusty said.

"Did you enjoy your time here?" Jacob asked Devyn.

"More than all the years I spent at my old office. Even when I was in the engineering design department and not where I am now," Devyn admitted.

"Really?"

Devyn nodded.

Perhaps Devyn would like it when I mention the job proposal from Jokul. This could work out for them.

"We'll see you at the Solstice event, Rusty," Jacob said.

"I'll be there," Rusty said with a wave and smile.

Jacob placed his hand on the back of Devyn's back and led him back through the workshop. Devyn cradled the globe close to his chest to not drop it and release the transmitter.

When they exited the building, the soldiers watched them.

"We're heading to CPD headquarters for the R&D office. Could you please alert them to our presence and travels? Agent Strike should be notified," Jacob said.

"Of course, Lord Serac," one soldier said.

"Thank you."

With their intentions secured, Jacob led Devyn across the complex toward the collections of buildings that made up the CPD headquarters. Instead of going to the main entrance, he veered down to another building.

"Lord Serac. It's so formal and disconcerting around here," Devyn said.

"Mostly the soldiers and Nutcrackers called me that. Anyone else calls me Lord Jacob."

"Why?"

"My position within the Frosts. One of the oldest that's still around. And I'm Jokul's direct line grandson and not removed a couple times. To many around here, that puts me in a higher rank, close to the Council. It's an honor title."

"I like it. Suits you," Devyn said and bumped their shoulders.

Jacob tapped him back. Then they reached their targeted building. A small sign designated it the Research & Development Department of the Cheimon Patrol Division, NPD Center.

The soldiers nodded to him. "Lord Serac?"

"Yes, and this is my crystal partner, Devyn," Jacob said.

"Agent Strike is waiting inside to escort you to R&D."

"Thanks," Jacob said.

The soldier opened the door to allow them entry.

"All this will go away—" Devyn asked while they walked inside. He looked all around, but he kept his tight hold on the globe.

"After we deal with the threat from the Lads. Usually the Center is friendly, peaceful, and filled with joy," Jacob said.

"I would like to see that."

"We can visit whenever you want since you can pass the Artic barrier."

"Greetings, Jacob, Devyn. Devyn, how are you enjoying your time in the NPD? Not what you expected, right?" Strike asked while he walked down the hallway toward them.

"Hel— Greetings, Strike," Devyn said, corrected himself to the Cheimon's preferred greeting. "Definitely nothing like the stories and songs, but I believe I prefer this version. Without the threat of danger hanging over us."

"We need to take care of this problem and things will turn around. The Christmas spirit and joy will take over everything after the Winter Solstice. So much that you'll want to run away and never return," Strike said.

"Like when stores have Christmas items up for sale and it's not even Halloween," Devyn said.

"Worse." Strike chuckled. "Good to see you up and about, not woozy or confused."

Devyn laughed. "Feeling much better. Learned a lot with Rusty. We discovered the transmitter. Plus, I no longer want this watch anywhere near me." He held out the globe and golden watch on his palms.

"I can take them from you and make sure they're kept safe."

"Thank you."

Strike scooped up both items into one large palm. "Thank you for coming up with the idea of a transmitter in the watch. That was quite brilliant."

"It was the obvious answer when Jacob said no one could get through his barriers unless invited. How else could someone find us?"

"Still, quite brilliant. The R&D elves will be giddy when they see this," Strike said. He turned and led them down the hallway.

"Don't know if I ever visited their main area," Jacob said.

"It's quite an amazing display they built in there," Strike said while he pushed on one of the swinging doors. "The gloriousness that is the R&D master environment."

Jacob chuffed a laugh and entered with Devyn.

"Wow," Devyn said while he tried to take in everything.

Jacob let out a low whistle.

"This is only the lobby," Strike said with a chuckle.

There were monitors along the walls. Three different stations filled with tablets, equipment, piles of paperwork, and busy R&D elves. Directly in front of them was a long, high raised bar of sorts that separated them from the immediate stations. Three elves sat there.

"What happens here?" Devyn asked.

"This is the intake area. This group of elves and fairies will collect all the items, listen to the information, label and designated to a specific section of the department. There is an initial inspection that takes place at those stations to deem the safety and priority levels," Strike said. "After that, it's assigned a case number and taken to the main sections for further investigation and discovery."

"Greetings, Strike, what do you have for us this time?" one of the elves asked. He placed a silk covered tray on the counter.

"Greetings, Cedar, something our friend discovered in the ensorcelled watch along with the Tinkerer, Rusty. The transmitter was inside the watch. It allowed the Lads to track our friend, Devyn, anywhere, even through a Frost dimension and warded shield," Strike said. He placed the globe and watch on the tray.

"Interesting bits you have. This is one major case you and Lord Jacob discovered. Keeping all the elves and fairies on their toes to figure out everything you brought to us," Cedar said. He lifted the tray and placed it in front of him. Then he worked on his end of the procedures. "Any spells on the transmitter?"

"Rusty sensed some leftover magic, but doesn't believe there's an active spell. He suggested something minor that allowed it connect to the Lads for location and time," Devyn said.

"We'll evaluate it."

"Excuse me. Are there any updates from Alabaster on the progress with the Frost crystal partners?" Jacob asked.

Cedar glanced up and nodded. "Alabaster dropped off the earlier globes for evaluation. Then gathered a larger group, globes, and supplies. He assigned everyone out to cover the names on a list. They portaled out about five minutes ago. I know Alabaster was going to a place in Spain first. Other than that, there is nothing."

"Thank you."

"Of course. It might take several hours to reach everyone upon the list and perform what tasks they need."

"Understood."

"Anything else?"

"The FVI elf maid with the necklace?"

"Still in processing and investigation. Though we can connect the spell upon the necklace to the one on the watch."

"Thank you again."

Cedar nodded and went back to work. "I will notify you when we learn everything, Agent Strike."

"Thanks, Cedar." Strike turned to face the couple. "That's it for now. We can't go any further because there is high-level security clearance beyond that next set of doors. Without it, we stay here in the lobby in front of the counter. Even agents can't pass through the doors unless an R&D elf or fairy is with them."

"We can tell you that all of the spells and the needle point back to the Lads. Everything is covered in their magic and touch. There is a definite touch of the sorceress, Grýla, on all the spells. Her energy makes them long-lasting and pinpoints the spell directly upon the connection tendrils between the Frost and their crystal partner," Cedar said.

"Mama always has the oomph," Strike said.

"Icicles," Jacob said. He gathered Devyn close and hugged him.

"Grýla?" Devyn asked, but didn't break Jacob's hold.

"Ancient ogress who studied sorcery. She uses black magic to camouflage her appearance," Strike said. "She's considered mama to the Yule Lads. All thirteen of them."

"Yikes. One of those ancient tales that is actually true?"

"And even worse than you could imagine. The tales came from Iceland and they were trolls. Like most immortals, their appearance adjusted over time from trolls to men. Still, they remain powerful men," Strike said. "If you can call them that. I wouldn't."

"Not the first time they attacked. Not the last. Every single time we stop them from getting anywhere near the Center and the Beacon. This will be one of those times," Jacob said.

"Exactly. How about we get together tomorrow? Go over the plans with the Nutcracker lead, Toy Soldiers leaders, and the Mouse King wants in on the action. Lord Kringle and Lord Jokul will attend the meeting. I'm not sure if Mother Nature will be there," Strike said.

"I wanted to spend time with—" Jacob paused.

"Don't even think about it. You meet him and learn how to kick Yule Lad ass. For us. For what that bastard did to us," Devyn said.

"Are you—"

"I'll hang out with Rusty again. I like it there."

"Dev—"

"Don't do it. You figure out how to kick Yule Lad ass. Got it?" Devyn waved a finger at Jacob's face.

Jacob blinked once, slow and steady, at Devyn's insistence.

"Wow. I'm impressed," Strike said. "Go, Devyn."

Jacob rolled his eyes.

Devyn smirked. "He understands."

"Yes, yes, Devyn. I will figure out how to kick Yule Lad ass," Jacob said.

"Good. Now... Please take me shopping. I want to check out those stores," Devyn said. He patted his fingers on Jacob's cheek. Then he headed toward the entrance.

"I definitely like him. A lot. He's a good one. Wish I could find one like him," Strike said in a low tone. He bumped his fist against Jacob's shoulder.

Jacob grinned. "Yes. I like him too. A lot."

"Will send a message through your house elf about times. Go have fun with your guy tonight. Forget about the Lads. Repair your relationship with him. Fix your crystal. We need you at full strength for the Solstice," Strike said.

With a nod, Jacob moved toward Devyn. He kissed Devyn on the temple. At the same time, another crack healed within his crystal. Then he rested his hand on Devyn's lower back and walked off with him.

· · · ·

WALKING DOWN THE SIDEWALK, they passed multiple teams of soldiers on patrol. Many Center-based villagers scurried past, their eyes darted all over, as if they expected danger to strike them down. At times, the Nutcrackers stepped forward to calm the residents with a few words.

"Just until Solstice. All of this chaos until the ball, right?" Devyn asked, but he kept his tone low.

"Hopefully, we'll finish it at the ball, if not before. Depends on how things go down," Jacob said. "No matter what, nothing will happen to you. Understand?"

Devyn nodded.

"Now. What shop would like to check out first?"

"A bookstore."

"Bookstore? Why?"

"Need to catch up on my history. The real stuff. Rusty recommended a few books."

Chuckling, Jacob linked their arms and went down the sidewalk. "Best place to go for that is here." He paused and opened a door. A bell jingled their entrance. "Welcome to The Holly Leaf."

They entered the welcoming and cozy shop filled with deep evergreen wooden shelves filled with books of all colors, sizes, and covers. Soft twinkling lights wrapped around the exposed beams. More direct lights connected to each top shelf. Stuffed armchairs for a little reading strewn in perfect nooks. The window was decorated with books, holly, lights, and the shop's two calico cats curled together while they napped. Off to the side was a simple desk with an old-fashioned register. An old elf stood behind the desk. He had a pointed beard that touched his chest and nose-clipped glasses perched on his nose. He wore a holly-green vest with a holly pin and a cherry red and white striped shirt. The desk hid the rest of his outfit.

The elf adjusted his glasses and smiled. His green eyes sparkled. "Greetings and good evening, young fellows."

Devyn jabbed a finger in Jacob's side at the greeting.

"Greetings. You're the proprietor, correct? Pine Holispirit?" Jacob asked.

"That's me." Pine adjusted his glasses. "Oh, good cookie crumbles. You're Lord Jacob. My apologies."

"No offense, honest. This is my crystal partner, Devyn."

"Greetings, Lord Devyn."

"Lord?" Devyn asked.

"By honor tradition of your relationship," Pine said. "How can I assist you?"

"I'm new to the Cheimon and the Dimension. Do you have any histories a newcomer could read and understand? I'll be attending the Winter Solstice Event with Jacob and don't want to make a fool of myself or him. I spent time with the Head Tinkerer, Rusty Magicmoon, and he recommended a few titles." Devyn listed three different titles.

"History. Along with a customs and mannerisms book. I have everything you need, including those three books. They are quite popular so I always have them in stock. Stay here. It'll be easier if I collect the books. Perhaps you can browse at a safer time," Pine said.

"It's another reason we're here in the Dimension and I'm not doing my job," Jacob said.

"Rumor is the two of you along with a CPD agent helped figure out what is happening to the Frosts and what could happen to the

Dimension," Pine said. He adjusted his glasses again. "Are the rumors true? Could the Lads attack the Solstice event?"

"There's the possibility," Jacob said.

"Should I attend the event with my wife?"

"You will be protected against any danger. And your presence will bolster Lord Kringle's magic and energy."

"I have never missed a Solstice event. I shall not miss this one, Lord Jacob. Now, those books. Yes. I have what Lord Devyn requires. A few simple reads to give him all that he needs before the big event," Pine said and scurried off through the wooden shelves.

"I don't think I want to shop anymore after this place. The situation kind of ruins the high of shopping," Devyn muttered.

"Understand. I'll check in with Mistletoe about dinner," Jacob said and pulled out his thin ice tablet. He tapped a message to his house elf.

With moments, the tablet chirped back a reply.

"Dinner will be ready in three hours. Normal around here. Unless you're hungry?"

"Had cookies most of the day."

"How about a cup of hot cocoa?"

"I could go for that."

Jacob tapped another message. "I'll tell him to stick to schedule and we'll be home soon."

"Home. I like the sound of that."

"Really? There's something I would like to discuss with you when we go home."

"About what?"

"A potential change to things. I'll explain in private."

"Of course. Secrets of the Frosts," Devyn said in a low, teasing tone. He wandered over to the window, placed his fingers by the cats.

The calicos opened their crystal green eyes, sniffed, and rubbed their heads against their fingers. Soft purring filled the room.

Jacob smiled.

"Here we are. Just what you need. Ahh, looks like you have been accepted by the felines. Excellent judges of character," Pine said when he reappeared out of the stacks.

"It was all right to approach them?" Devyn asked.

"Of course. Of course. They like to greet guests."

"Oh, wonderful," Devyn said and returned to the desk.

"I presumed you didn't require anything about the Frosts, not that there are many published tomes on the subject," Pine said. He carried five books in his arms. Each one a different thickness and color.

"Secrets of the Frosts," Devyn teased.

"Shush, you," Jacob teased back.

Pine chuckled while he circled the desk and placed the books down. He pulled one and held it out to Devyn. "To prepare for the event, I recommend you read this one first, Lord Devyn. You have a house elf, Lord Jacob?"

"I do. Mistletoe Jangle."

"Ahh, an excellent young elf. He can assist you with any questions or practice. There are multiple guides and scenarios. Mistletoe can help create them for you," Pine said. "It's quite a fun experience."

"Looks like I'm not visiting Rusty tomorrow," Devyn said.

"You can always stay home," Jacob said.

"Ahh. No, I'm not going to hide away. I'm staying at your side if you need to face the danger, but I can visit with Rusty after I practice." Devyn checked the books and glanced to Jacob. "Can we take all of the books?"

"Of course. Pine, please place everything on my account," Jacob said.

Pine pressed buttons on his register and printed a receipt that Jacob signed. "Shall I have a sleigh deliver the books?"

"No, we'll take them," Jacob said.

With a smile, Pine packaged the books into a holly green bag with the shop's logo splashed across the front. He finished with a bright red ribbon and a holly leaf combo. Then he handed the bag to Devyn. "Enjoy the books."

"Thank you for everything," Devyn said. "A pleasure to meet you."

"Same here. I hope to see you both at the event." Pine waved them off. "Come back and visit anytime."

"Have a pleasant evening," Jacob said and escorted Devyn out the door and back down the street.

They strolled down the sidewalk and stopped at a sidewalk café, Chocolatehat Café.

A fairy smiled and met them. "Greetings. Would you like a table inside or outside?"

"Outside. Please," Jacob said. He glanced at Devyn. "Trust me to order?"

"Of course," Devyn said.

Turning back to the fairy, Jacob ordered, "Two cups of dark cocoa with extra whipped cream, marshmallows, and chocolate shavings."

"Right away, Lord Jacob. Please have a seat over there."

Jacob guided Devyn to a table and held out the seat. Devyn settled in the chair and slid the first recommended book out of the bag to check it out. He set the bag on the extra seat. Jacob sat next to him and waited for the questions.

Within moments, a waitress brought out their mugs of hot cocoa. She placed a mug in front of each and added a small plate of peppermint sticks and spoons in the middle. Jacob gave her enough dominion pennies to cover the cost and tip. The waitress smiled and checked on the other patrons.

Instead of asking questions, Devyn kept his nose close to the book. He muttered something about needing a highlighter.

"Can't magic that up. The R&D teams haven't figure out that one. I'm sure there are some back home," Jacob said.

"Huh? Oh. Yeah. Sure," a distracted Devyn said. Then he picked up the mug and sipped. His eyes popped wide when he caught the taste. Then he stared at the mug.

Jacob hid his smile behind the mug.

"This is delicious!"

"One of the best here." Jacob tapped his pinkie to his lip.

"What?"

"Whipped cream mustache."

"Oh. Will lick it away later. Too good to waste a drop," Devyn said and continued to sip.

"I could take care of that." Jacob held up and wiggled his finger. "Or in a more intimate fashion."

"Uh-uh. It's all mine." Devyn licked his upper lip to catch the white foam deliciousness.

"Stingy."

Laughing, Devyn lifted his mug and sipped.

More cautious, Jacob scooped and stirred the marshmallows and cream into the dark chocolate. Then he picked up a peppermint stick and swirled it into the chocolate for another layer of flavor. He sipped again and nodded in satisfaction at the minty coolness mixed within the deep, rich dark chocolate and cream.

After finishing their cocoa, Jacob tugged Devyn close to exchange a cocoa-whipped cream kiss. Devyn chuckled and played along.

Leaving the café, Jacob hailed another sleigh taxi to carry them home.

Entering, Jacob looked around while he removed his jacket and hung it up. A toasty fire roared in the fireplace. Candles lit and placed in different groupings. A random NPD-based show played on the television for soft background noise.

"Mistle? We're home," Jacob called out.

"In the kitchen," Mistle called back.

"We'll leave you be then," Jacob said.

"Another half hour and we can eat," Mistletoe said.

"We just had cocoa. No treats. Promise."

"Good!"

Shaking his head at his house elf, Jacob turned to help Devyn out of his jacket and hung it up. Then he bent and removed his boots. After motioning for Devyn to do the same, he placed them on the drying rack. He stepped into a pair of cozy house slippers.

Jacob slid his hand into one of his jacket's pocket and pulled out the crystal. He carried it to the coffee table and laid it on a velvet cushion.

"Ooh, my slippers are here. Yay!" Devyn slipped his feet into the slippers. Then he carried the bag to the sofa and settled down. He unpacked the books, placed them on the table, and picked up the one he started reading at the café.

"I'll find a highlighter for you. The clicker is on the table. Sometimes we can get mortal channels, but there are Dimension-special channels," Jacob said.

"Okay," Devyn said.

Jacob went to his office. He grumbled at the stack of folders and tablet the FVI team dropped off. Knowing he couldn't get away from his work, he gathered them up along with the highlighter and a pad of sticky notes.

Returning to the sofa, he settled on a cushion near Devyn and placed his things on the table next to the stack of books. He held out the highlighter and notes to Devyn.

"Ooh! Thanks. Pen?"

Sighing, Jacob opened one of the coffee table drawers, rooted through the slight chaos, and unearthed a pen. He clicked it and scribbled on a folder to see if the ink flowed. When it did, he handed it to Devyn.

"Thank you. Figured I would read, gather ideas, flag stuff, and go over everything with Mistletoe tomorrow."

"Good plan."

"Don't want to overwhelm the poor elf."

"Umm. Might be the other way around. Especially with Mistle. He tends to go way beyond the basics, so be warned and feel free to tell him to pull it back." Jacob turned on his tablet and leaned back to read the emails and messages from his FVI teams spread throughout the northeast.

Devyn twisted a little, moved Jacob's arm, and leaned against Jacob's side.

"Comfy?" Jacob asked while he glanced down. He adjusted his arm so he could at least work, but at the same time allow his fingers to play with Devyn's golden hair.

"Yes. Wait—" Devyn tugged the throw blanket across his lap. "Ahh. Even better. Perfect. I didn't realize how much I missed our quiet nights spent like in this position. Something to change and bring back."

Shaking his head with a smile, Jacob went through his messages and answered the different FVI members. With a touch of concentration, he sent out extra bursts of power where it was needed.

"Hey. Wait a minute." Devyn lowered his book. He adjusted his position to look back up at Jacob. "You were going to tell me about something when we got back here. What was it?"

"Oh, yes, forgot. Thanks for reminding me. Got lost in my work," Jacob said.

"Ha! Shoe on other foot. It's usually me."

"Well, this is my busiest season."

"True. Now that I know what you mean. What were you going to tell me?"

Jacob explained about the growing building in the Center and Jokul's offer.

"Does this mean we could remain here full time?"

"With visits to the mortal realm when you desire."

"What would I do?"

"There are options for you. I know Rusty would want you in the Tinkerer shop. Though, you might find a place with me at the new headquarters."

"Lots to think about."

"Exactly. I told him the same thing. I'm not going to make a final decision without your input."

"Right away?"

"No. We have time. It's a big decision."

"We'll figure it out," Devyn said and settled back against Jacob's shoulder. He picked up his book and continued to read.

Leaning over to place a kiss in Devyn's golden hair, Jacob felt another crack heal within the crystal.

Chapter Eleven

After a lengthy planning session, Jacob could only hope they figured out all the holes and possibilities in their layers of protection and attack. Even with the awakened Frosts, Jokul appeared a touch tired because none of them could connect a new crystal to a partner in such an abbreviated time.

Pacing a bit, Jacob worried his hands together. He tried not to touch the beautiful velvet and silk outfit Mistletoe created for him. The silk was an elegant silver shirt with an airiness to it. A midnight blue silk cravat tied around his neck. A midnight-blue velvet created the vest and pants. There was a delicate frosting of ice and flurries creating a lacy effect across the vest and pants. Then there was the long velvet and leather duster in the same midnight blue with more of the lacy frosting of ice and flurries all down the shoulders and back. The outfit was finished with a pair of supple silver boots.

"Would you stop fussing?" Mistletoe said while he walked down the steps. He moved to Jacob, slapped his hands apart, and circled him to tuck and smooth. "If you need to shift to your Frost persona, the outfit will not be damaged. It will reappear after you pull your energy back and return to Jacob."

"Thank you for that touch. I'm sure I will need all of my Frost magic and energy tonight." Jacob held still under Mistletoe's attention. "Did my item arrive from the jeweler? I can only pray he finished my request in time. I know he's been booked solid for the event."

Mistletoe sighed and snapped his fingers. A jeweler's box appeared on his palm. He popped open the top to reveal the gleaming crystal nestled as the center of a delicate snowflake.

"It's perfect. Will it work with his outfit?"

"Yes, he's wearing the opposite of you. Here he comes..."

Jacob looked up the stairs and felt his jaw drop in surprise.

Devyn walked down the stairs. He trailed his fingers in a graceful fashion along the banister. As Mistletoe said, Devyn wore almost the opposite of Jacob's outfit. His ankle boots, pants, and vest were a silvery velvet. His cravat a silver silk. His shirt was a midnight blue silk. Instead of a long duster, he wore a silver leather hip-length coat with midnight-blue velvet accents. The lacy accents dusted across the velvet accents instead of the entire outfit to signify his position as a crystal partner to a Frost. His sunflower gold hair was soft and flowing around his face. He finished the look with a touch of eyeliner and mascara to bring out his deep blue eyes. A flicker of silver powder caressed his cheekbones.

When he reached the floor, Devyn turned and posed.

"Absolutely magnificent. You're the most handsome crystal partner," Jacob said. He passed the box back to Mistletoe in a surreptitious way. Then he walked over to him. He carefully cupped Devyn's face and placed a gentle kiss of adoration and love upon his mouth.

Devyn held Jacob's shoulders and returned the kiss. He pulled back and checked out Jacob. His eyes darkened further with arousal and appreciation of Jacob's appearance. "You look gorgeous. A powerful Frost."

"Thank you. I have a gift to finish your look even more. Plus, it will tell everyone who you're connected too," Jacob said and accepted the box again from Mistletoe. "Devyn Risher, will you accept my crystal heart and become my partner?" He popped open the top to reveal the specially designed setting for the event.

Devyn's eyes widened when he saw the pin. He nodded slow, tears brimmed and glistened against his dark eyes. "Oh, yes, Jacob, yes." He kissed Jacob.

"Thank you, my love," Jacob said and plucked the pin from the satin bed. He set the box aside. Then he carefully pinned his crystal to Devyn's lapel against his heart. For an extra touch, he sent a burst of magic into his crystal to make it glow and glisten throughout the night. The crystal was seamless and true.

"No more cracks in the ice," Devyn whispered.

"No. No more cracks."

"The sleigh is here," Mistletoe said. He swirled a silver and blue cloak around his pale blue and silver outfit that matched them in a subtle way. Then he pinned it with a special triple snowflake pin Jacob designed and gifted to him.

Jacob held out his arm to Devyn, who curled his hand around Jacob's elbow. With a sigh, he held out his other elbow to Mistletoe, who laughed and placed his hand on Jacob's elbow.

"Come along, my gentlemen," Jacob said and led them out the door. Sideways so they all fit.

Mistletoe snapped his fingers to close and lock the door.

At the end of the walkway, Jacob helped them into the sleigh. Then he climbed in after them. He secured a blanket over their laps, as Devyn curled in close.

Without a word, the driver clicked to his reindeer pair and set off for Kringle Hall where the Winter Solstice Event took place. It was the heart of the Dimension and the location of the Beacon, hidden deep within the Hall which only appeared for the Solstice.

Soon their driver joined a line of other sleighs in the massive circular driveway around a central fountain with an elegant design of the three eternal figures who created the entire Dimension and Beacon. Eternal water flowed from all three forms, but it didn't freeze.

When they reached the double staircase that lead to the massive doors with marble banisters and statues decorating the exterior, a cherry red dressed elf strode to their sleigh. He snapped his heels together and bowed. "Greetings and welcome to the Winter Solstice

Event." He held out his hand to assist Mistletoe and Devyn out of the sleigh.

Jacob paid the driver and climbed down on his own. Though he flipped the elf a few coins.

"Thank you, Lord Jacob. Enjoy your evening," the elf said. After another bow, he slipped the coins into a pocket and hurried to the next sleigh.

Jacob held out his arm to let Devyn slip his hand into the crook. Mistletoe waved him off and followed them up the stairs. Mistletoe snapped their invitations into existence to present to the door guardians, a pair of massive rock trolls, dressed in leather finery. Multiple teams of Toy Soldiers patrolled the exterior along with their Nutcracker officers.

After inspection, the trolls waved them through.

They followed the crowd toward the massive ballroom where the entertainment happened for the Dimension. At one end, raised above the floor in an elegant box, the Council sat upon their thrones. Each throne decorated according to their own magic. Attentive and protective Nutcrackers placed on either side. The rest of the Kringle family were in a box off to Kringle's left side. On the same side, the eldest of each reindeer line had a box for them. On the other side, in a similar style of boxes were the Frosts. The first box remained empty for Jacob and his little family.

On the opposite side of the floor was a stage with a Cheimon orchestra and small choir playing music to entertain the crowds.

During the event, the Beacon would magically appear from its hidden place at the center of the dance floor.

"What do you think?" Jacob asked closed to Devyn's ear.

"It's magical and beautiful," Devyn said. He lifted his hand to catch one of the magical snowflakes floating through the air only it dissipated the moment it touched his warmth. "How—"

"Magic," Mistletoe said. He paused to remove his cloak and exchange it for a ticket. He fluffed his thinner evening jacket and cravat. "I'll meet you at the box."

"Don't get into too much trouble. When Lord Kringle makes his announcement, I want you—" Jacob said.

"In the box with Devyn for protection. Got it," Mistletoe finished. He wiggled his fingers and danced away into the crowd.

"Dancing the night away," Devyn said.

"Whenever he gets a chance. Still enjoying having him around," Jacob said. "Ready to greet and mingle? Remember what our dancer elf taught you?"

"Mingle away. Pray my memory holds true."

Jacob kissed Devyn's knuckles, placed Devyn's hand back against the crook of his elbow. Then he led him away through the crowd and introduced him around.

A couple of hours later, they settled into their box. A fairy stopped by to offer them a plate of nibbles and cups of sparkling cider, ice wine, or hot drinks. Jacob chose a hot cider while Devyn went for the ice wine. They set the plate on a small table between their chairs.

"May I join you?"

At the Spanish accented voice, Jacob rose and turned. "Darío! What are you doing up? You should be resting and recovering."

The Spanish-based Frost shook his head, though he seemed a little weary and heartsore. "I couldn't rest anymore. Built my new crystal. Recharged. I know I'm needed here for the possible battle. Jokul recalled all of the strongest Frosts from their posts to position themselves here."

"Which means you should—"

"Emelina didn't accept my new crystal," Darío said. "The R&D elf, Alabaster, hand delivered a letter from her. Something about the spell clearing her mind. She moved out of our home and took the children with her."

"Oh, Darío..." Jacob gathered Darío in his arms and held him tight.

"Thirty-seven years. It was more than a crystal partnership. We were married. She started the proceedings." Darío cried into Jacob's shoulder while he returned the hug.

"I'm so sorry, my brother," Jacob said.

Darío pulled back, wiped the tears from his eyes, and tried to regain his control. "Of course, foolish me, I thought all was well between us. She wasn't happy. Not anymore."

"You were together a long time. Even for mortals, that's a long time together." Jacob curled a hand around his half-brother's cheek. "You'll find someone new. Someone special who can appreciate you and your gifts."

"We Frosts have no choice but to find someone to care for our crystal. It's part of the package deal when we accept Jokul's offer," Darío said. He shrugged and glanced over. "Introduce me, brother."

Jacob turned and held out his hand.

Devyn rose and walked a couple of steps to meet them.

"Darío Escarcha, please meet my crystal partner, Devyn Risher," Jacob introduced. "Devyn, this is my half-brother and the Frost of Eastern Europe, Darío."

"Greetings. A pleasure to meet you," Devyn said.

"Greetings and well met. It is truly an honor to meet you," Darío said and motioned to the lapel pin. "I see your crystal is healed, brother."

"It took some time—"

"And the truth to come out. But we did it together," Devyn interrupted.

The Frosts chuckled.

"Plus, I'm not a simple mortal anymore," Devyn said.

"Correct. You are Cheimon."

"Forty-two percent. Guess that's a big deal," Devyn said.

"I thought I was the first, but according to the records, Emelina had a small percentage," Jacob said.

"Under ten percent. She could never join me in the Dimension. One of the other issues that often cropped up between us. I learned while my children could become Frosts, none would be strong enough to survive the change. I lost..." Darío stopped talking and shrugged it off. "No more sadness tonight. There is a gala to enjoy."

"And time to kick some nasty Lads asses," Devyn said.

Darío laughed. "Indeed, dear crystal partner, indeed."

"Come and join us until that happens," Devyn invited.

"Thank you. I didn't feel like sitting alone in my box," Darío said and accepted one of the extra chairs. Then he picked up a couple of nibbles when Devyn offered the plate. He waved to a passing fairy server and ordered a cup of hot cocoa. "Need the sugar hit."

"There's plenty of sugar to go around," Jacob said.

They waited out the evening.

Strike slipped into the back of the box and appeared on Jacob's far side, but kept to the shadows. "Greetings, Jacob, Darío, Devyn."

"Update?" Jacob asked.

"They're here. Three Lads slipped in like we wanted. Multiple minions are with them, dressed to resemble elves and fairies," Strike said. He held out an earbud. "Place this in your ear. You can hear and talk to the team. Krieg is watching everything on the monitors."

Jacob accepted the bud and tucked it into his ear. "This is Jacob. Testing connection."

"Got you loud and clear, Jacob. Who's the handsome fella next to Devyn? It ain't you," Krieg said and teased.

"Be nice. That's Darío, the Spanish Frost."

Darío glanced over when he heard his name and Jacob shook his head.

"He's cute."

"Krieg—"

"Okay. Okay. Minions are on far side of room, by the pillars. Lads in the back, between the stage and entrance. They're waiting."

"Keep the soldiers and Nutcrackers back. Warn the Mouse King."

"Already done. Awaiting orders."

"Hold. Wait for Kringle."

"Got it."

Jacob nodded to Strike. "He's got them."

"I'm moving to the Council box."

"I'll protect the Beacon."

With a nod, Strike moved to the front of the box, placed a hand on the barrier, and hopped over it. He landed on his feet and moved through the crowd toward the Council box. He entered around back and leaned to speak with Kringle and Jokul.

At the same time, a cheery, slightly tipsy Mistletoe entered the box. "Ooh, greetings, everyone. Galas are so much fun."

"Straighten up. We're on alert," Jacob said.

Mistletoe grumbled about losing his tipsiness, but snapped his fingers. A small tonic bottle appeared. He popped the top and drank the sparkling contents. Then he made the bottle disappear. It took a few seconds, but he let out a soft burp. "Okay. All good."

"Protect Devyn. That's your only job. It'll be dark magic."

"I have enough fairy in me to counteract it. Devyn will be safe."

"Darío, with me. Can you create enough magic?" Jacob asked.

Darío rose from his chair and nodded.

"Good. Stay with me. Do whatever you can to assist me. We protect the Beacon at all costs. That's our job along with any extra Frosts."

"Understood."

Jacob nodded and rose to remove the long coat. He draped it over his chair. Then he rolled up the sleeves of the flowing silver shirt. Finished with his preparations, he leaned against the wall by the low barrier. His eyes scanned the massive room.

When the orchestra rattled their drums and ceased the music, all patrons turned to face the Council box. Lord Kringle dressed in his finest white velvet suit with fur trimmings were matched with a wide black belt and knee-high black boots polished to a high sheen. A silver and diamond-crusted buckle finished the belt. A matching hat topped his snow-white hair.

"Greetings and welcome to all! Welcome to the Annual Winter Solstice Event. A night of music, dancing, and the renewal of our magic," Kringle called out with magic to boost his voice to carry throughout the cavernous room.

The crowd rose with cheers. Sparks shot up with magic. They burst into bits of light and snow. It caused more cheers.

Kringle held up his hands to calm the crowd. They responded immediately to him.

"The Solstice moon rises high in the sky upon us." Kringle pointed a hand toward the ceiling and a special skylight rolled back to his magical call. "Behold the heart of our Dimension, the North Pole Beacon!" He lowered his hand toward the floor.

Mist rolled across the floor while a circle of Toy Soldiers moved in to open the space in the center of the room. They firmly pushed the crowds back, away from the center.

Then, through the mist, the red and white striped Beacon rose and stood straight and tall. A massive forever ice diamond topped the pole and glistened under the lights.

The crowds joined hands and danced in circles while the orchestra played the ancient Winter Solstice song. The choir sang the lyrics written by their ancestors to welcome the Solstice moon.

The glowing blue light became stronger while the moon slid into position to fill the window and poured into the massive ice diamond. The diamond glowed and splintered the light across the room.

"Minions and Lads on the move," Krieg said in all the ear buds.

"Let them move. Put up shields on all boxes," Strike ordered.

The invisible plasma shields created a soft 'whoosh' when engaged and they covered the front opening of each box. A soft fluttering of light flickered as concentric circles rippled out from Jacob's fingertip touch. According to R&D, they could pass through the shield from their side, but not from the exterior.

"Great Winter Solstice Moon Spirit, revive our Beacon, fill it with your beautiful magical light so it may sustain our beloved Dimension—"

"Blah. Blah. Enough with this boring display," a different booming, sinister tone rang out to interrupt Lord Kringle. "Now!"

A different shout of anger and rage echoed. Slim sinister creatures rushed and pushed through the crowds toward the boxes and the Beacon. They ranged in size from massive trolls to small gnomes. Their disguises melted while they revealed their true selves to the crowd.

One Lad stormed directly to the Beacon. He raised a hand to shoot a blast of dark magic.

Before anyone else reaction, Jacob hopped the low wall, pushed through the barrier, and raced to the Beacon. He shouldered his way past the fleeing crowds and straight through the soldiers, who raised their weapons and brandished them against the massive Lad.

Pulling up all the magic he could possibly create, Jacob transformed into his Frost persona. His skin became blue. His hair pure white and spiky. His elegant outfit became brown pants torn at the knees, bare feet, a flowy white sleeved shirt covered in snowflake embroidery, and a deep brown vest covered in an ice and snowflake pattern. In control of his magic, he poured it into the thickest column of ice around the Beacon to protect it from the incoming blast. "Come on. Come on. Come on."

A couple of soldiers cried out when the dark magic struck them. Another strike winged Jacob's shoulder.

Calling out in pain, Jacob spun away from the Beacon. His bare feet couldn't find traction upon the marble floor. He dropped to one knee and fought back the pain. Blue-tinged blood spread across his snowy shirt.

"Jacob!" Devyn cried out through the mass hysteria growing.

"Cheimon patrons, retreat to the stage and exits! Nutcrackers, Toy Soldiers, Mice Army, to arms! To arms! Anyone with intense light magic to the forefront! We fight for the Beacon! We fight for the Dimension!" Kringle called out. He leaped out of the Council box with Jokul and Gaia next to him.

Nutcrackers surrounded them along with the most powerful team of fairies, who had the most concentrated form of light magic.

"Frosts to the Beacon! All Frosts to the Beacon! Assist our brother," Darío called out.

Jacob twisted to keep one hand lifted to grow the column of ice. He grimaced through the pain and weakening power.

"We're here, Jacob, we're here! Medic!" Darío called out.

"No. No. Create a massive open column around the Beacon. From the floor to the skylight. Ice. Snow. Ice. Snow. Ice. Snow. Thick layers. As thick as we can possibly make," Jacob ordered. "The rest must fight back the Lad! Don't let him through."

A fairy medic somehow made it through the chaos. With a few quick movements, he assessed the damage. Gloves protected his hands from Jacob's blue skin that could freeze anyone's skin that came in contact with it. "It's almost down to the bone. Dark magic lingers."

"Slap a bandage and let me get back to work."

"Not with this injury. Give me a chance to help you so you can continue the fight. Otherwise you will collapse."

"Do it." Jacob held still for the medic.

The medic cut the snowy white sleeve. After using one bottle to flush out the lingering dark magic from the wound, he used another bottle of healing liquid. He added a few flakes of polar snow to assist the healing liquid. Then he wrapped a bandage around the wound and tied it off. "Do you need a boost?" The medic held out a hand.

With a nod, Jacob placed his hand in the medic's hand and accepted a boost of magic from the fairy. It revived his energy and pushed back the pain. "Thank you."

"Protect the Beacon," the fairy said and rushed off to find his next patient.

Toy Soldiers and the Mice Army fired upon the minions — the trolls and gnomes. Their weapons armed with a nickel-based bullet infused with polar snow that could enter through any dark defensive barrier and armor. The teams of fairies concentrated their attacks upon the Lads, along with the gathering Frosts.

The Council also used their combined magic to attack the Lads.

Until the front entrance doors banged open and slammed into the walls.

"Oh, sweet balls of lightning!" Krieg said.

"What happened?" Strike asked.

"It's her. Grýla. And someone I presume is Victor Merrowynd is by her side."

"They're for the Council to confront and attack. No one else can withstand her magic," Strike said. "What's happening outside?"

"The soldiers and mice are fighting back the minions. They're keeping the worse at bay. We have to deal with what got inside."

"Got it. Everyone, keep it up," Strike ordered. "Not quite to plan, but we have all exits covered."

"Kringle. Kringle. Kringle, come out. Come out. Your precious barrier is weakened. We are here to take control," Grýla called out. "Oh, Jokul, how tired you appear. Your poor Frosts." She laughed long, low, and sinister. Then she patted Victor's cheek. "Such an excellent son of mine. He discovered the perfect hidden attack."

"Aye, thanks to my wretch of a partner," a Scottish Frost, Alastair, said in his ancient Scots' accent. "Come on, Jacob, on your feet."

"What are you talking about?" Jacob asked while he waited for the potions to kick in and return him to full-strength.

"Long story short, since there's not much time," Alastair said. "My partner was dying of cancer and in hospice care. This sweet young lady charmed herself upon my partner and me throughout those difficult months. When my partner passed, she offered. Lost in grief, I gave it to her. Wasn't until Alabaster appeared and discovered the dark shadows in my crystal. He went a step further and analyzed her blood. She's the granddaughter of Merrowynd. Placing her under a truth spell, he got her to admit how she hacked into my tablet and downloaded a list of all the crystal partners. It set off all that happened. It was all due to my wretched mistake, lost in my grief."

"Not your fault."

"It was—"

"Not the time."

"Right. Time to kick ass."

"Get me back to the Beacon."

Alastair assisted Jacob to his feet and back to the Beacon.

"How many layers?" Jacob asked.

"On the fourth," Darío said.

"Two more. At least." Jacob spun and discovered one of the Lads pushed through enough and raised his hand. "Hit the ice!"

Everyone dropped in time. They all watched in fear and horror as another vicious strike of dark magic blasted the Beacon's barriers. The outer snow column crumbled and flew into dust. The ice column held.

The Lad hollered in anger. Two more Lads tried to race through his side for another hit.

"More columns! Hurry! Ice. All the way," Jacob said. He poured his magic through his body and created the barriers of ice.

Multiple fairies appeared through the crowds. They added their own light magic to the ice to strengthen the barriers.

Another roar from the Lads announced the next attack.

The fairies threw up more protective shields, but everyone dropped and ducked out of the way.

The strikes hit the columns, but this time, everything held.

The Beacon continued to charge under the bright moonlight of the Solstice Moon.

Jacob dropped back to one knee, drained of energy. He watched the others build one last column of ice and fairy magic.

Then everyone turned to face the Lads and minions.

At the same time, the Council combined their attacks upon Grýla and Merrowynd. They knocked them back multiple times to Grýla's surprise. She hollered when a strike sliced across her hip. The Lads abandoned their attack upon the Beacon and raced to their mother's side.

Jokul stepped forward. He moved his arms, called upon every ounce of his power and energy, and shoved a massive wave and storm of snow, ice, and wind at the Lads and their mother. Kringle and Gaia followed the attack with their own bright magic filled with their light and energy.

Then Jokul created a massive portal back to the Lads' dominion. Using his wave, he pushed them all through the portal. Once the last Lad tumbled backward into the portal, he snapped it close.

Seeing their leaders disappear, the minions scattered toward all the exits in a mass exodus.

"Let them flee. Have teams follow to make sure they leave the Dimension and return to their dominions. Plug all the holes and leaks," Strike ordered through the buds.

When they were sure the last minion left, Jokul turned and waved to the Beacon. The columns dissipated in clouds of flakes and sparkles. The Beacon poured its pure light through the somewhat darkened room.

Crowds of patrons streamed back into the event hall from wherever they hid during the battle. They cheered for their Council, the Frosts, and all the teams who fought to save everything they held dear.

"Barriers dropped. All is calm. Shutting down," Krieg said.

"Jacob!"

Turning at his name, Jacob saw Devyn shoving his way through the crowds. Mistletoe right behind him. He held out his arms. Pulling back his Frost persona to protect his crystal partner from potential harm, he returned to his regular Jacob appearance and the once elegant outfit. It was now ruined in similar patterns as his Frost outfit.

Devyn slammed against him, almost tackled him to the ground. He wrapped his arms tight around Jacob.

Their mouths came together in a desperate kiss.

All strength poured back into Jacob at Devyn's touch and love.

Crowds cheered and clapped around them at the wonderful display of love and the strength of a crystal partnership.

The Frosts cheered and called out to Jacob and Devyn.

Devyn pulled back, braced Jacob's face between his hands, and stared at him. "Tell Jokul you accept his offer. We're staying here. Where we belong."

Jacob blinked. This wasn't what he expected to hear from Devyn. "What?"

Devyn laughed and kissed him again. "You heard me. I love you so much. No more cracks in the ice. We belong here. Together."

"Love you back!"

"Not getting rid of me."

"Nope, never. I'm keeping you forever."

"Good. Didn't like my job anyway."

Laughing, Jacob tugged Devyn back into a hug. He even lifted Devyn off his feet and twirled him around to everyone's delight.

"I take it you're both staying," Jokul said.

Jacob looked at his grandfather and smiled. "Yes, Grandfather. Like Devyn said, it's where we belong. No more cracks."

• • • •

The End

To be continued in Cheimon Tales #2: Strike's Stand

Cheimon

Anyone with bloodline/genetics from NP Dimension, only with those over 25% can enter the North Pole Dimension barriers

Cheimon Bloodlines:

Claus

Frost

Elves

Dark Ælf

Fairies

Reindeer

Nutcrackers

Toy Soldiers

Mouse Kingdom

Cheimon Patrol Division (CPD)

Headquarters based in the Center, anyone of Cheimon bloodlines can become a CPD Agent/Tech/Support, they control, follow, and protect the Dimension Beacon and the Naughty & Nice Lists, Agents and supporters are spread throughout various bases around the globe for ease of access/research/reconnaissance

Eternal Snowflakes

Magical flakes with the potential to become anything and power spells

Frost Scions

Each scion helps control and maintain the Winter Spirit magic around the globe

Certain areas require more scions than others, each scion creates an ice crystal heart – can adjust to many sizes and styles – and present to a chosen partner during a Winter Solstice. A partner's lifetime can stretch out and increase with the heart's power and the scion's level of power/magic. If cracks, the scion has time to repair a relationship or chose another partner. If shatters, the scion loses touch with humanity, returns to the NP Dimension and a special Frost Cavern for an icy sleep – 50-100 years. A heart can be replaced only 5 times before the scion turns into a permanent ice sculpture, but this can vary based on the scion.

Flakes, Verglas & Ice Department (FVI)

A collection of Flakes, Verglas and Ice elves and fairies who assist Frosts to organize and control the chaos that was a winter system

Glass Snow Globe

Can become a portal or container

Grýla

The Yule Lads answer to her, their Mother, a powerful ancient ogress and sorceress of the darkest powers, predates all legends, and ruler of the northern Russian mountainous region they inhabit

ID Kit

a CPD kit with a flexible strap to tap and analyze blood for traces of Cheimon

Jack Frost

Definitely not the cute little magical elf in the stories, there are 8 Jack Frosts created by the Spirit of Winter, to blend into the mortal population to sire future scions, Frosts, to help control and organize the aspects of winter

Naughty & Nice Lists (N&N List)

Old fashioned lists of stories are computerized and detailed oriented while the global civilization grows, The lists musts remain within balance to maintain the Dimension's magic and power.

A special beacon alerts CPD agents to research, track, and locate suspicious behavior, appearance, and reactions in subjects/objects and figure out how to return this 'beacon' subject to balance

North Pole Dimension (NPD or Dimension)

The physical pole is the anchor of another dimension created by the first NPD Council to protect those with the bloodline to live and work. Mortals were becoming far too curious, even more so with various space and ground technology. It covers the entire Artic Circle, which is the boundary line, between the mortal and the NP Dimension. There's an invisible barrier that if someone crosses it, the barrier will determine their bloodline. If a scion of the Dimension, they will enter it. If not, they will remain within the mortal realm.

NP Beacon

The very center and beating heart of the Dimension, in the mortal realm an actual pole, and a version of it in the Dimension realm. Every Winter Solstice, the magic is renewed with energy and magic by the Solstice Sun. The Cheimon magic comes from the beacon. Without the renewal, the beacon is in danger of weakening, dropping the barrier, and revealing us to the mortal world.

NPD Council

Kringle Family – Claus scions of first Santa, Ded Moroz
Spirit of Winter - Jokul Frosti
Mother Nature – Lady Gaia

NP Dimension Currency

Dominion Pennies – copper-ice coins, 100 coins equal 1 silver

Lunar Silver – silver-ice coins, 10 coins equal 1 gold
Chrono Ryal – gold-ice coins
Credit – per person or household

Polar Snow

Eternal snow gathered directly around the actual North Pole and imbued with potent magical power

Research & Development (R&D)

Headquarters based in the Center, Elves and Fairies run the lab/workshop, creators of Tech and Supplies used by the CPD and Frosts

The Talvi Cheval

Magical free-standing mirrors with a silver frame engraved with reindeer, snowflakes, and evergreens. A user will press certain engravings, speak the location and name, and power to open the mirror and connect. Can speak and view through the connection. Can be used within any NPD or Frost dimension, unlike modern electronics.

The Yule Lads

Dark Magic scions, scions of the original 13 ancient Icelandic Trolls, that stole things, caused trouble, and scared mortals into behaving, now turned to more modern concerns and dangers, can enter the Dimension, but not the Center

Winter Drug Cocktail

combination of holly berry, mistletoe, chamomile, and lavender

Winter Solstice Event

A magnificent ball that happens in the Center during the Solstice when the Beacon is renewed with energy and magic by the Solstice Sun. Everyone looks forward to the event, dress in their finest, and dance and dine the night away

Nicole Dennis

Dreamy...Sensual...Forever Love

A quiet one, Nicole Dennis is the penname of an asexual author of different genres of fiction – both LGBT+ and hetero. Lots of characters, worlds, and stories build up in her head until she must get them down on the screen – anything from romance to fantasy to paranormal.

During the day, she works in a quiet office in Central Florida, where she makes her home, and enjoys the down time to slip into her imagination. She is owned by a new feline companion – a house panther, affectionately known as Brat Cat.

Contact & Media Info:

Facebook: www.facebook.com/NicoleDennis.Author

Facebook Page: https://www.facebook.com/NicoleDennis.Musings/

Facebook Group: https://www.facebook.com/groups/nicoledennis.author/

Website: http://nicoledennis.net

Email: nicoledennis.author@gmail.com

Twitter: @NDennis_Author

Amazon: https://www.amazon.com/author/nicoledennis

Goodreads Profile: http://www.goodreads.com/author/show/2791975.Nicole_Dennis